COWGIRL FALLIN' FOR THE RANCH HAND

BRIDES OF MILLER RANCH, N.M. BOOK 2

NATALIE DEAN

DEDICATION

I'd like to dedicate this book to YOU! The readers of my books. Without your interest in reading these heartwarming stories of love, I wouldn't have made it this far. So thank you so much for taking the time to read any and hopefully all of my books.

And I can't leave out my wonderful mother, son, sister, and Auntie. I love you all, and thank you for helping me make this happen.

Most of all, I thank God for blessing me on this endeavor.

AND... I've got a special team of advance readers who are always so helpful in pointing out any last minute corrections that need to be made. I'm so thankful to those of you who are so helpful!

OTHER BOOKS BY NATALIE DEAN

CONTEMPORARY ROMANCE

Miller Family Saga

BROTHERS OF MILLER RANCH
Miller Family Saga Series 1

Her Second Chance Cowboy

Saving Her Cowboy

Her Rival Cowboy

Her Fake-Fiance Cowboy Protector

Taming Her Cowboy Billionaire

Brothers of Miller Ranch Complete Collection

MILLER BROTHERS OF TEXAS
Miller Family Saga Series 2

The New Cowboy at Miller Ranch Prologue

Humbling Her Cowboy

In Debt to the Cowboy

The Cowboy Falls for the Veterinarian

Almost Fired by the Cowboy

Faking a Date with Her Cowboy Boss

Miller Brothers of Texas Complete Collection

BRIDES OF MILLER RANCH, N.M.

Miller Family Saga Series 3

Cowgirl Fallin' for the Single Dad

Cowgirl Fallin' for the Ranch Hand

Cowgirl Fallin' for the Neighbor

Cowgirl Fallin' for the Miller Brother

Cowgirl Fallin' for Her Best Friend's Brother

Cowboy Fallin' in Love Again

Brides of Miller Ranch Complete Collection

Miller Family Wrap-up Story

(An update on all your favorite characters!)

~

Copper Creek Romances

BAKER BROTHERS OF COPPER CREEK
Copper Creek Romances Series 1

Cowboys & Protective Ways

Cowboys & Crushes

Cowboys & Christmas Kisses

Cowboys & Broken Hearts

Cowboys & Second Chances

Cowboys & Wedding Woes

Cowboys' Mom Finds Love

Baker Brothers of Copper Creek Complete Collection

CALLAHANS OF COPPER CREEK

Copper Creek Romances Series 2

Making a Cowgirl

Marrying a Cowgirl

Christmas with a Cowgirl

Trusting a Cowgirl

Dating a Cowgirl

Catching a Cowgirl

Loving a Cowgirl

Marrying a Cowboy

Callahans of Copper Creek Complete Collection

KEAGANS OF COPPER CREEK

Copper Creek Romances Series 3

Some Cowboys are Off-Limits

Some Cowgirls Love Single Dads

Some Cowboys are Infuriating

Some Cowboys Don't Like City Girls

Some Cowboys Heal Broken Hearts

Some Cowgirls are Worth Protecting

Some Cowboys are Just Friends (Coming August 2024)

Though I try to keep this list updated in each book, you may also visit my website nataliedeanauthor.com for the most up to date information on my book list.

CONTENTS

1

Cassidy

"$\mathcal{J}$'m going in the house for a minute," Charity said, tossing the frisbee over to Cass with a nod. "Be back in a bit."

"Don't rush on our account," Cass said, catching the flying disc and sending it right towards Savannah.

The second eldest of the New Mexico Millers had never been overly fond of frisbee before, but she was plenty fine with it currently. It was easy enough to stand still or sit in her chair and still have a meaningful game with Savannah, who seemed to have hooked herself up with some sort of eternal energy source considering how long she could run around, cartwheel and do everything else that her skippy little heart wanted to do.

"Here," Savannah said, throwing the frisbee back, then taking off backward. "I'm gonna go long!"

"Alright, but not too long. I'm still a little shaky."

"You're the steadiest shaky person I've ever met," Savannah yelled back as she ran, and if that wasn't about the most Savannah-like compliment she could have given.

"Thanks for your assuredly accurate medical assessment."

"My dad is a doctor, you know."

"Ah yes, that lovely degree transference I've been hearing about. You ready?"

"Yeah. Throw it!"

Steadying herself, Cass did her best to give the young girl a long throw. She hadn't been out of her wheelchair and walking on her own for long. And she'd been able to throw and catch things for an even shorter time, so there was still a mental checklist she had to go through to make sure she didn't end up on her own butt.

Her butt that was considerably less muscular and padded than it was before her accident.

Cass grimaced and her sidetracked thoughts had her throwing wide, the frisbee arching far more to the left than it was supposed to.

But Savannah, being Savannah, dashed forward and jumped *way* further into the air than she had any right to and caught the neon pink disc right out of the sky, cheering as she landed. Cass found herself laughing too, clapping her hands as she congratulated the young girl on her catch.

Cass liked Savannah and admired her athleticism. But there was an undercurrent of melancholy to it as Cass remembered just how much she used to be able to move around.

It seemed like the time before her accident was an entirely different life, one where she was Charity's right-hand man and a general strong woman about the ranch. She could rope a calf, drive a fence post, work any of their machines and hand

Charity whatever tools she needed while also lugging around her sister's incredibly heavy toolbox. Sure, she wasn't Clara's level of lean, muscled body, but she *was* tightly layered with hard-earned grit.

Or... she had been.

Then everything had changed.

"Cass! Catch!"

That snapped her back to attention, and she clambered out of her own head just in time to see the disc flying to her right. For being such a young, wiry thing, Savannah could really *throw.*

It was like instinct, her body moving quickly to snatch it up before it could hit the ground. It was too much movement, too fast, and her mind screamed at her to abort the mission, abort, *abort!* But the next thing she knew, she was straightening just fine with the frisbee in her hand.

Whoa... had she just... bent? And turned? And also shuffled quicker than an old woman stuck in molasses? Impossible. She couldn't have, and yet...

"Whoa! That was so cool! I didn't know you and Dad had gotten to that level of movement yet."

"Neither did I," Cass said with a giggle bubbling its way out of her throat. An actual giggle. What if... what if she pushed a little more? Just to see what she could do.

Shuffling forward a little, she whipped her arm back harder than she would have just moments earlier, then launched it forward.

Cass tottered a little, her weight wanting to go much farther forward than she meant, but she managed to catch herself and stand upright again.

Huh, physical therapy really was starting to kick in.

It was a little slice of victory after so much can't, can't, *can't,* that *maybe* she got a little drunk on it. But it was hard not to, considering that the most she usually did when she was actually on her feet was to just stand there and not fall over.

And it was *fun*. Really solid fun that got her blood pumping and her cheeks hurting from smiling so much. Savannah was having a blast and so was Cass, laughing and sweating and calling out to each other. It was brilliant, the most fun she'd had in ages.

Until it suddenly wasn't.

It started with the frisbee just slipping past her fingers, and her smooth and steady bend down to the ground. The moment she stood, dizziness swamped her, and her mostly sure footing stumbled.

"Are you alright?" Savannah called, sounding like she was so very, *very* far away.

Cass wanted to answer, but her tongue was hanging heavy in her mouth. She just wanted to... wanted to what? And why were her legs shaking so much?

"Hey, I gotchu, I gotchu. Let's get you to your chair, okay?"

Skinny fingers were gripping her arm and supporting her at the small of her back. Blinking hazily, Cass realized Savannah was beside her. How had the small girl moved so fast? That didn't seem possible.

"I was fine," was all Cass managed to get out. Because she had been. She'd been more than fine. So what had happened?

"Yeah, but now you're not, so come on, your chair is right over here."

Cass nodded, and even that made the world go a little wobbly. She really had been alright. Sure, a little unsteady, and yeah, her ankles were always weak and her reflexes were slow, but she'd been *alright*. She *had*.

"We're almost there. We're almost—"

And then one of those suspect ankles went, rolling like it was disconnected from the rest of her body and sending both of them pitching to the side.

Savannah tried to keep her upright, that Cass could tell, but there was only so much the reedy girl could do. The injured woman hit the ground hard, and the spinning decided to ramp itself up, apparently.

"Miss Cassidy, are you alright?"

Cassidy Miller wanted to answer, really. She hated the panicked tone in the young girl's voice or the idea that she was scaring her. But there wasn't much Cass could do; everything was slipping away into a sort of kaleidoscopic soup with fuzzy black all around the edges.

"Miss Cassidy, I need to know if you can hear me, okay? I'm not strong enough to get you up."

Cass's gaze flicked over to the girl, taking in the Picasso-like arrangement of her features and how they twisted in concern. She would like to answer, really, but her tongue wouldn't move and her brain refused to supply the words that her mouth would need to work out anyway.

The Picasso-face didn't like this, and Cass was vaguely aware that it began calling for help. Calling for Charity.

Oh man, Charity was going to be so ticked at Cass for messing up, and that was the last thought she had as she sank into the swirling pool of colors that had been waiting for her.

WHEN CASS WOKE UP, she felt like she'd been laid out in a football field and gone over with a steamroller. Every part of her ached, sore and heated like she'd pulled all the muscles in her body then decided to rub salt in them for extra measure.

She laid there a moment, completely motionless because even breathing hurt, but eventually her eyelids weakly fluttered open.

And somehow that hurt too. How unfortunate.

She wasn't sure what she expected when she finally looked around, maybe the angry and concerned face of her sister over her while Cass was sprawled in the grass, maybe the interior of an ambulance, but it wasn't really for it to be her room, Charity quietly sketching something into her notebook by Cass's bedside.

"Hey there, how are you feeling?"

Internally, Cass had been braced for her sister's ire. Although Charity would never be outright aggressive with her, she had no problem telling Cass when she was being reckless or pushing herself too far. The eldest of the Miller clan was fiercely protective that way, and Cass didn't begrudge her that.

But that didn't mean that it felt so great when Cass disappointed her bigger sister. Or stressed her out. Although Charity would probably never admit it, losing their mother had left her with some control issues. She needed to make sure everyone was safe and taken care of to feel secure. And Cass wasn't complaining about that, not at all. She understood it. Losing their mother had been... traumatic, to say the least, and they all developed their own coping mechanism. Papa had his garden. Charity took care of everyone. Cassidy was her right-hand woman and go-getter. Clara was the domestic with a flair for the animals, and Charlie was the easy-going one who did whatever, and usually just happened to be there.

The only one who didn't have a... a *thing* was the youngest, Cecilia 'Cici' Miller. As it were, it was looking like she'd be the only one of the siblings to stay and get a full-on bachelor's degree in the great wild yonder.

But surprisingly, Charity didn't lecture her at all. She only had a look of concern on her face as she set her notebook down and crossed to Cass's side.

"Do you want some water? Alejandro said you might have a wicked case of dry mouth."

Shoot, they'd called Dr. Lumis? He was going to have some strong words for Cass during her next therapy session about her type-A personality or whatever. When she'd set her seemingly permanently single older sister up with the handsome doctor, she hadn't thought about the consequences of having both of her care providers—although in very different aspects —together as a couple. Much harder to get away with things.

"Yeah," Cass croaked, watching her sister uncertainly. But she just picked up the pitcher at the bedside and poured a glass, sticking a straw in it—where had that even *come* from— before handing it off.

Cass took it, sipping through the straw gratefully, and *wow*, that certainly did feel good.

"Cass..." Charity began about mid-long sip.

There it was.

"Yeah?" she responded cautiously once she swallowed.

"Savannah told me that you two were just playing, but the way she described it, it sounded like you weren't using your walker and you were doing a lot of bending and standing back up."

"That might be an accurate assessment of what happened."

It was the hurt look on Charity's face that *really* made Cass feel bad. Well... worse. She was still shaky and nauseous from the whole losing consciousness thing.

"Cass, I know this whole thing grates at you, and I know that you've been working so, *so* hard for months for all these tiny gains, and that could be frustrating, but you have to stay vigilant. Did you even realize that you hadn't eaten breakfast and that's why your blood sugar dropped low enough for you to pass out?"

"Oh, is that what happened?"

"*Cass.*"

"Uh, no. I thought I ate so I could take my pain medication."

"Clara said you made yourself a bagel, with lox on it too, good choice, but got distracted by Savannah arriving and left it on the counter."

"I suppose that's ringing a bell now that you mention it."

Cass hadn't meant to. She tried to be responsible about feeding herself since she had so much more movement than she used to, but clearly, she'd dropped the ball.

Charity pulled the chair closer, sitting right up against Cass's bed and gently gripping her hand. "I am endlessly impressed by how strong you are, really. But I need you to be *careful.* I know you understand why."

Cass licked her lips, feeling a bit of nerves rise up in her. "I will, be careful that is, I promise. I really was just caught up in playing and having fun. I have been taking it easy lately, like really, I have."

"I know. And I know what I'm asking you isn't entirely fair and that I have no idea what it's like to have to go through all the things you're going through. But please, Cass, I can't lose you too. And maybe I'm being overly paranoid, but seeing you laying there on the ground... it... it was *bad*, Cass. I don't want to ever see that again, okay?"

Her voice was gentle the whole time, vulnerable, but that made it worse than a stern lecture. Charity asked for so little, and that was just for Cass to take care of herself, and she couldn't even manage that.

"I will. I promise."

Charity nodded, smiling softly, and it was a nice expression to see. Charity had spent the last handful of years clearly going through the motions, and it had pained Cass just how wounded her elder sister was from that awful ex-husband of hers, Eric. *That* guy was a real selfish whack job, and once Cass got full use of her body back, she was going to give him a piece of her mind.

And by piece of her mind, she mostly meant a piece of her fist. Or maybe even shovel? She would figure it out.

Charity gave her hand a squeeze. "Thank you, sis. Really. Now, do you think you're up for some soup? Clara's been in a tizzy since, you know, so she made up a whole thing of that spicy one you like so much."

"Clara made tortilla soup?!"

"Yup. So she's definitely in one of her moods. I wouldn't be surprised if I go down there to find her making a roast and about five different pies. Or maybe an impromptu bonding session with all the kids."

"I guess getting antsy is a Miller thing, isn't it..."

"At least in our branch, it is."

Charity chuckled and stood, refilling Cass's glass as she did. "I'll be back soon. Just rest up."

"Roger-wilco."

She left and Cass settled, thinking that would be it, until she realized that there was another form leaning against the doorway.

"You're full of it, you know that, right?"

Cass stared blankly at her little brother, Charlie. He was standing there with his classic grin that she knew made so many young women swoon but mostly just made Cass want to give him a real strong noogie.

"Come again?"

"You're real good at buttering Charity up, but if you really wanted to be good for her and heal, you'd stop trying to keep being who you were before you were hurt. You'd stop pushing yourself with Savannah, stop trying to do as many chores as you can and let Clara n' me actually *help* you."

"Yeah, like the two of you don't already have full plates. Especially since it's *summer*. You know it's all-hands-on-deck, but you want me to just... what? Sit around?"

"Yes! Exactly! Your only responsibilities should be your hygiene, feeding yourself and your physical therapy. We're your family, Cass. Let us look out for you."

"I do! But there's a line, you know." There was something definitely off-putting about her little brother telling her what to do. And also... that a little voice in the back of her head was agreeing with him. "Charity drives me to all of my appointments or takes me anywhere when I just want to get out. Clara helps me with stretching and gives me massages when the muscle pain is just awful. I can't even take a bath on my own!

"I ask *so* much of all of you, and you want me to pour on *more*? There's only so much I can ask you guys to do!"

But Charlie just rolled his eyes. "If you really think that, then just hire someone."

"What?"

"Hire someone. There are plenty of seasonal ranch hands you can find or you could get a caretaker. You certainly have the money or the insurance for either."

"I hadn't thought of it."

"Well maybe you should. Look, I know you've been handling most folks' worst nightmare and have been dealing with it like a champ, but I also feel like you're playing on hard mode. You've got all these advantages and resources, things that a lot of people could never dream of having, so use 'em, okay?"

Cass didn't say anything for a long moment. Her natural response was to tell her little brother to butt out, but while he was generally an easy-going, go with the flow type, that didn't mean he was childish. It was... it was just hard not to see him that way sometimes.

"I will think about what you've said. Do some research."

"Good. Then it won't feel like you're lying to Charity all the time."

"I'm *not* lying to Charity?"

He scrunched up his face and gave her *such* a sibling look. "Aren't you though?"

Maybe she would have argued further, but he just gave a cheeky little salute and headed off. Even with him gone down the hall, his words lingered behind him.

Hire someone, huh? Now there's an idea...

_____

2

Mick

$\mathcal{M}$ick pulled up to one of the side pumps at the small gas station, pleased that his RV had a place to fit. That wasn't always a guarantee in small towns and he'd certainly had to get... inventive before when it came to refueling his method of transport. Even with his oversized tank, he had to stop more often than the average driver, considering just how old his rig was and the fact that he was hauling Othello's heavy self and his trailer along too.

Sliding out of his vehicle, he went straight back to the horse trailer in question, opening the top section of one of the doors. Othello huffed at him, reaching his nose out, no doubt expecting some sort of treat. The big guy was fine, of course. Mick had spent quite a lot of money in addition to doing labor trades with an electrical handyman to make sure his horse had working AC and a watering system in his lil' trailer. That way the southwestern heat didn't bother the horse. Several folks had told him that interior horse fans or a bucket would be enough, but maybe that was how *they* wanted to treat their horses. Mick was more than happy with his choices and was already planning his next move to spoil Othello.

"I'll go see if they have apples or bananas inside. Sorry that I let us run out."

Othello gave him a suspicious look and Mick could only chuckle. His mount was a very handsome fellow. A Belgium draft horse with russet tinged brown fur and a black mane with matching tail and feathering along his lower legs. He was a draft horse, and a truly big one at that. Not really meant for riding, but he was Mick's horse and right-hand man none-theless.

"I'll be back. Behave now."

Not that Othello ever really misbehaved. He was one of the most chill horses that Mick had ever met, which was probably why they got along so well. Mick had too much to do and too many dreams to accomplish to be worried about drama or anything of the like.

Locking the trailer back up, he headed into the gas station. It was much cleaner than some of the small town, hole in the wall stops he'd been to, and for that he was grateful. It also was surprisingly well stocked. He'd been to some out-there stations that had only cigarettes and lottery tickets, neither of which he was interested in.

It was relatively smooth sailing for once to grab a couple of drinks, a snack he didn't need, some toilet paper, then pay for his gas up front. Considering he already seemed to be on a roll, he decided to ask the attendant a question—always a risk considering that gas station employees seemed to range from absolute saints to some of the rudest people he'd ever met, with few in between. Thankfully, the good far outnumbered the bad, but boy, that minority of cranky ones managed to stick out.

Or maybe he was still salty about the time one had called the cops on him for 'stealing a horse' except the horse in question was Othello. *That* had been such an awful, unneeded, and dangerous situation.

"Hey, is there a notice board around here or in the town yonder? Or anything like that where I could look for work?"

He didn't necessarily *need* to land a gig. He had been in an alright position after he left his last job when the urge to travel became too powerful to ignore, and he still had plenty of funds to last him. But after a year and a half of making his way further and further west, taking odd jobs here and there as he desired, he was getting that urge to build up his nest egg again.

It was a pretty constant cycle with him and had been ever since he'd gotten away from the city. Find a seasonal or temporary farming/ranch job, work as hard as he could, save up tons, then move along as soon as the itch to travel got too demanding. It worked for him, even if many of his employers were sad to see him go.

"Sure. We have a bulletin board next to our grocery store. Right on Main Street if you want to drive into town."

"Thanks, I appreciate that."

"No problem. There's always work to be had in the summer. Between the three farms, the one ranch, the carpentry shop and the road workers, there's plenty of gig or seasonal positions that should suit you right well."

"Well that's good to hear, I have to say. Sign of a healthy town."

"We do our best here," the cashier said with a smile that

did indeed seem genuine. That boded well for the general nature of the place.

"You have a good day now."

"You too, sir!"

With a tip of his head, Mick finished up his purchase and headed out. It always lifted his spirit when the first person he met in a place was amiable. Goodness knew he'd met plenty that weren't.

"Alright, big guy, ready to find our new crashing space?" Othello just gave him a flat look, which made Mick chuckle. "Yeah, yeah, you'll be able to stretch your legs soon. I've got a good feeling about this place."

Othello let out one of those skeptical breaths of his, but still took the treat that Mick offered. With another pat on the nose, Mick went around to the front of his camper and hopped in.

It wasn't hard to find Main Street. Not at all. In fact, the whole town had two main roads that formed a giant "X" and then everything else seemed to branch out from there.

Mick pulled up to the grocery store, glad it actually had a parking lot unlike some of the small towns he traveled through, and he just stood there outside of his vehicle for a moment, people watching and getting a feel for things. There were quite a few children in town, which meant it was growing, but also lots of faces of different colors. There were clearly white folks, some indigenous folks, a couple of Asian folks, and people who were ambiguous enough in between.

No other black people though.

Granted, Mick had only been standing there about ten minutes, not exactly a generous sample size. While it wasn't entirely unheard of for him to be one of a handful of black people in a town, he generally found that there were reasons so few folks like him chose to settle down in a place.

He would have to keep his eye out. Otherwise, he'd have to do his fade style haircut himself, and he was absolutely horrendous at it. Which was his excuse for why his hair was so unkempt at the moment. Long months on the road could do that to a man.

Satisfied with his mini-observation time, Mick headed around front to where he assumed the bulletin board would be. He'd almost fully rounded the corner when what felt like a padded wall *slammed* into him, nearly knocking him over.

"Whoa there!"

"Oh, my gosh! Are you alright?" a startled feminine voice greeted him, and he blinked for a moment only to see a giant of a woman standing not too far from him. She was only a couple of inches shorter than him, meaning she had to be over six feet tall, with broad shoulders and even broader hips. Mick took in her curvy form, but he made sure his eyes stayed on her apologetic face. He wanted to be polite, after all.

"I'm fine, ma'am. You had quite some momentum going there." He played it off with a laugh and the woman let out her own relieved chuckle. While Mick wasn't exactly the most socially tactile person, he was able to pull his charm out every once and a while. Especially around a beautiful woman who looked like she might be able to beat him in a fistfight.

"I have to say, I'm impressed you're still on your feet. Not everyone could'a done that."

He wasn't sure whether to laugh at the comment or not, but then she laughed, and it was such a happy, boisterous sound that he couldn't help but go right along with her.

"I'm glad you're such a good sport," she continued, a cheery smile about her ruby lips. She had a retro sort of look to her, one he wasn't used to seeing. "I was just in a hurry to get home because I've got several broody hens to deal with, but I'd promised my sister I'd make a run into town. So I suppose I was trying to speed run it."

"Broody hens? You know, what my nana used to do was freeze a water bottle and put it under her in her nest. The cold works like an off-switch, apparently."

"A frozen water bottle? Oh, I like that. I've been trying to fence them off from their nesting materials, and you can imagine how *that's* been going. Thank you so much for—" She cut herself off and stared at Mick for a good breath or two. "You used to farm life, mister?"

"I suppose you could say that. I've been working as a ranch hand and general help-about these past few years."

At that her face illuminated, and it was certainly a sight. "You wouldn't happen to be looking for a job, would you?"

3

Cassidy

"Hello! Cass! I got that mango gelato you wanted!"

Cass perked up at that, picking herself up from where she'd been sitting on the downstairs couch. She used to have to spend a pretty penny ordering the specialty dessert online—the trials of being lactose intolerant with a love of ice cream. But the general store in town *finally* started carrying it and she was *elated*.

That elation faded, however, as she realized that her sister, Clara, wasn't alone.

There was a man with her, and not just any man. He was a tall, dark drink of water just on the rugged side and entirely dashing with full lips and onyx eyes. Cass hadn't thought much about her appearance since the accident, but suddenly she found herself wishing she wasn't in her pajamas with hair she hadn't fixed in three days.

Shoot, she thought as she realized she wasn't even wearing a bra.

As subtly as she could, she hauled the blanket up to her shoulders, feeling her cheeks flush. Cass didn't exactly like non-family members seeing her not properly dressed.

"Mick, this is my sister, Cassidy Miller."

"You can call me Cass," she interrupted quickly, wincing at how sharp the comment sounded. She hadn't meant it that way; she was just rusty on social interaction. Other than Alejandro and Savannah, she didn't really interact with anyone outside of her family.

"Much obliged to meet ya, ma'am."

But Clara continued on in that honey-sweet way of hers. "Cass would be your boss, actually, as this independent contractor position is hers."

Mick looked from Clara back to Cass. "I'm more than happy to interview, or give you references. I do have an RV and a mount, however. Is there somewhere I would be able to keep them 'round here?"

"You can park on an unused part of our land, if you want, and you're more than welcome to use an empty stall for your horse. We expanded our barns but then decided to cut back on our horses. Only have about four of them now."

His face did something strange at 'only four,' but he didn't say anything. Was that good? Bad? She didn't know. She also didn't know why she was so thrown off right now. She wasn't so thrown when she met Alejandro. She'd even had the where-withal to try to set up the handsome doctor with her sister.

Well, at least that was going well.

Cass tried to focus on the conversation instead of the cowboy's good looks. "Your responsibilities will be pretty simple. You're basically assuming all my chores so I can concentrate on my recovery. And, before you ask, I'm hiring you because I don't want my siblings covering for me. They have enough on their plates already."

"...I wasn't going to ask, ma'am."

She wrinkled her nose at that. "Oh, please don't call me that. I'm way too young."

"Whatever you prefer, miss."

Well, that was better than ma'am, so she could live with it.

"Thanks. I'm more than happy to give you a tour of what I do, but it's pretty straight forward. My eldest sister handles mechanics, repairs and the like. Clara there, is good with the smaller animals, like the goats and chickens while my brother, Charlie, mostly tends to the horses."

"I see."

She didn't know why, but she'd expected more questions. More little goalposts to guide her commentary. But without any input from him, she found words tumbling out of her mouth in a torrent.

"So, there's a lot of maintaining the grass, being a secondary aid and errand-runner for anything Charity needs, helping father in the garden, then tending to our small crops. I'm kind of the jack of all trades here. Before my accident, I was adding some solar panels to the roof."

"Sounds like you keep busy."

"I used to."

There was an awkward sort of silence for a couple moments until Clara cleared her throat. "Alright, well I'll leave the two of you to it," she said with a polite tip of her head before walking to the kitchen. She was out of sight, but not so far that Cass couldn't call out if something went wrong.

"I'll try to keep you to forty hours a week or below, and I'm willing to pay three dollars over the going rate since this is just a temporary position and you can't set down roots."

"I'd certainly appreciate that."

"And I'm not sure if you have insurance or not, but we do have that available if you need. We find it's for the best considering we have a mini-not-quite-a-ranch here."

"That's awful generous of you."

"Just trying to do right by people. Can't expect you to give your all if we're not providing the protection for you to do so."

"Can't argue with that logic."

Cass took a deep breath and sat up straighter. "Hey, Clara, can you go grab the contract our lawyer put together for us? I printed it in the office."

"Of course. I'll be right back."

Cass glanced back to the ranch hand, giving him a longer look over. He was dressed in a casual plaid button-up with well-worn jeans and cowboy boots. He was both quite tall and wiry, almost the opposite of her eastern cousins, but it suited him. His hair was unkempt, as was his beard, but neither of those could obscure that magnificently regal bone structure of his.

He didn't seem to care or realize about his attractiveness, however, standing there in the middle of her living room, giving her eye contact when she talked but subtly looking elsewhere when she fell silent.

Cass wasn't a chatterbox, not like Charlie, but she found herself wanting to fill the silence. Like if she said enough, she would unlock some secret code that would have the man conversing like a normal fellow. She technically knew he was probably just the quiet sort, and yet... the feeling persisted.

Thankfully, once Clara returned, Cassidy had a clear and direct way to guide the conversation. Mostly it was rehashing what she'd already said, but it outlined things more clearly—especially when it came to holidays, hours and termination of the contract.

"Of course, this doesn't include room for your trailer or lodging for your mount, but I'm more than happy to update our lawyer on the specifics and have a new one to you by tomorrow."

"I would much appreciate that. There's a lot here to go over, so I'd like to take it with me and read over this tonight, if you don't mind."

"Oh, I don't mind at all. But would you like a tour of the place? Just to make sure it's right for you? We don't have a big place, and it's nothing compared to some of the other big ranches in our family, but it's too much for us to do with Papa getting older and me in this chair."

"Chair?"

At that point, she realized that she was sitting on the couch, her wheelchair tucked against the wall near the kitchen. Ever since she'd been able to kind of shuffle along with her walker, she'd taken to trying to distance herself from the thing. She appreciated all her chair did for her and everywhere she took it, but she also... resented it. It was a shining beacon and reminder of everything she had lost and was still struggling to regain.

...why, of all people, had that accident happened to *her*? What had she done to deserve her spine being almost shattered while her entire pelvis was pulverized?

"Ma'am—I mean, miss?"

He pulled her out of her sinking thoughts, and she cleared her throat. "Sorry, I was in an accident, and that's why I'm hiring you. I use a wheelchair to get around for the most part, but Charity is trying to devise plenty of ways to make more areas of the property accessible to me."

She knew better than to chase those lines of thought. It was one of the first things her therapist coached her on. She'd been resistant to going to a shrink at first. The whole profession seemed silly and self-absorbed to her. But after she'd yelled at Charity on her second day home, she'd immediately gotten herself a therapist that specialized in pain management as well as coping with loss.

Because, as much as she liked to forget about it, Cass had lost so much. Her freedom, her ability to just get up and go. And if her family wasn't already filthy rich, she couldn't even imagine how hard it would be. She was lucky, incredibly lucky, and yet sometimes she just wanted to *sob* over everything that was cruelly taken away from her.

"I see."

To her great surprise, the stranger's face didn't twist with pity or sorrow. He had an expression almost like he was... learning a math lesson, before nodding matter-of-factly. "That ramp outside makes more sense now."

"Ah, you noticed that?"

Another matter-of-fact nod. "It's very well made, but it's hardly worn, so I thought it was probably new. And now you've confirmed that. Did your sister, the eldest, make that?"

Wow, so he really was listening. "She did. Wouldn't let me help on it either."

"It wouldn't have been much of a present that way, I'm guessin'."

"Nah, probably not."

And that was it. He nodded yet again, and his eyes moved to the windows, as if he were taking in everything stretching out in front of the house. There wasn't much. Most of the gardens and everything was behind their modest mansion.

"It's funny," he said.

Cass waited several long moments for him to elaborate, but he didn't. What a strange guy. "What is?"

"Oh, sorry, I forgot to finish my thought. It's just funny how, in a lot of ways, this feels like some sort of homey cabin or hunting lodge. But in reality, the apartment I grew up in could fit in here about a dozen times over."

Cass afforded a small chuckle, trying to envision how an apartment could possibly be that small. "You're not from around these parts, I reckon?"

"Grew up in a city all the way back east. Been making my way across the south slowly but surely."

"Any destination in mind?"

This time it was just a shake of his head. "No, ma'am, just get the bug to start wandering, and so I do."

"I see. Well your career choice is probably pretty convenient for that."

"That it is, miss."

For someone being raised back east, he sure did have the drawl and the mannerisms of a southern boy, through and through. She found herself looking at his face again, as if she were trying to puzzle him together. Not that he needed puzzling, exactly, and yet...

"You mentioned a tour, miss?"

"Right, let's do that. Clara, could you bring me my chair?"

"Oh, don't worry, miss, I'll grab it."

Before she could tell him it was alright, he was up and over to the chair, unfolding it casually and rolling it to her, where he put on the breaks without her even asking. It was all *entirely* too natural, and she couldn't help but say something about it.

"You seem to know your way around one of these things."

He paused as he finished putting on the second break before chuckling ever so slightly. And *wow*, was that a sound.

Cass thought that most talk about the 'joy of laughter' was cheesy and overwrought, but suddenly, she very much was changing her mind. It was a low sound, and rumbly, but there was a sweet sort of bashfulness to it that lit all the way up her back and made the hair on her neck stand up.

That... that was weird.

"I didn't even realize. But yeah. I was raised by my nana, and she used one of these since I was seven, pretty much."

Raised by his grandmother? She was in a wheelchair too? Cass greedily gobbled up every shred of info and tucked it into her brain. She didn't know why she was acting like knowing tidbits of backstory about her possible hire were important, but she was too busy chronicling it all to question it.

"Did you have any brothers and sisters?"

A voice interrupted their conversation. "Oh, did you call me?"

Cass nearly jolted out of her skin. Her head jerked to the kitchen, where Clara was standing with two bottles of water in hand.

"I handled it, miss. We were just about to go on a tour of the place."

"Wonderful! Do you mind if I come along for part of it, Cass? I need to tend to the chickens and goats as it is."

"Sure, sounds good to me."

"Great. I'll fetch another water bottle and be right with you."

True to her words, Clara grabbed herself her own drink and then they were all heading out.

It wasn't exactly a quick tour, not by a long shot. Even with all of Charity's work, there were still several areas they had to go around or maneuver through. And much like his interview, the stranger was relatively taciturn as they went along.

It wasn't abrasive, or rudely so, but he would speak usually only when addressed or when he had a question. And if he *did* have a question, they were brief and to the point. He also didn't inquire about her family, their wealth, or even their name. Although they weren't celebrities, by any means, most of the people in their small town were well aware of who the Millers were and their long, *long* legacy.

Granted, it would take him less than a five-minute search on the internet to figure out half of that, but only if he thought to actually search the internet.

Eventually they made it back home and Clara dismissed herself again. She'd ended up sticking around the whole time instead of wandering off to tend to her animals, and Cass had more than feeling that her sister had only used that as an excuse to keep an eye on her without Cass feeling babysat.

"So, as long as you don't find anything objectionable on your overnight read of the contract, I'd like to offer you the position."

The cowboy seemed surprised, his eyes going wide for a moment. "Are you sure?"

"I am. If Clara trusted you enough to bring you to the ranch, then I trust her judgment. We're close like that." She also didn't want to mention that she dreaded letting a stranger into their home and something about the Mick character put her slightly at ease.

But only slightly. Part of her felt all ruffled up and intrigued for reasons that made absolutely zero sense.

"Well, I reckon I could stick around for a while. Provided you don't have anything about selling my soul in that contract."

What!? A joke! He'd made a joke! She winked. "I'll have to have the lawyer strike that out."

There was that chuckle again, rumbling and low. "Please be sure you do."

"Awfully demanding, aren't you?"

"What can I say? I may not have much, but I'd like to keep what I do."

"Well, maybe as a bonus we'll decide to extend the contract."

"I look forward to it."

He offered his hand out for a shake, and she took it, handing over the contract once they were done. She tried not to note the callouses across his palm, and the small jolt of... *something* she felt at the touch of his skin. "You're more than welcome to find a spot for your RV and tend to your horse in the meantime. We can meet up back here tomorrow, if you'd like."

"I can certainly do that, miss. Thank you again, for this opportunity."

He wandered off to where his RV was parked right next to the truck. Cass watched until he got in. Strange guy, that was for sure, but not so strange that he wouldn't fit in. Besides, he was just a temporary contractor. He'd be around for three months and then she'd be well enough to do most of her chores all on her own.

...even if her doctors thought her timeline was much too optimistic.

4

Mick

"There's my good man. Feeling better, now that you've been out for a while?"

Othello nickered at him, most likely telling him to get back to the brushing and less with the chatting.

"Hey, I am perfectly capable of multitasking."

His mount gave him a look that told Mick exactly what the animal thought of *that*, and he couldn't help but laugh.

"You're lucky you're such a looker because your attitude is horrendous. I am the hand that feeds you, you know."

Othello waffled and shook his head, his mane shimmering and bouncing around him.

"Yeah, yeah, and you know it too," Mick said, rolling his eyes before continuing to brush his best guy. They'd both had a long day, but who could have guessed all the good that would come from it?

Sure, the Miller Ranch was one of the smallest operations he'd ever been hired for, hardly a ranch. But since it was a family-run place, it made sense that one sibling being side-lined could put them so drastically behind in several respects. And he had no doubt Cassidy did plenty of work. He'd only met two of the Miller sisters, but they were both clearly physically built, with broad shoulders and hands that spoke of years of work. Sure, neither of them were hard on the eyes at all, but that wasn't something he should notice about an employer.

Still, those Miller genes didn't seem to be hurting.

Even with how much her accident had clearly taken a toll on her body, Cassidy's form exuded a feminine sort of strength that reminded him of an athlete or Olympian. Although her hair was cut incredibly short, that somehow accentuated her womanly features. With thick lashes, full lips and high cheekbones, she could have been a model.

Not that Mick had noticed.

Because he hadn't.

Well, sure, maybe he'd noticed, but he hadn't thought about it since.

... or at least not very often.

But, even with a painfully attractive boss, he couldn't lie that he was leery too. Although he'd met plenty of amazing, lovely people in his journey, he'd also met plenty of not-so-lovely people. And as a black man dealing with rich, usually white folks, he needed to be careful.

It wasn't that everyone was racist. It was that there was just no way to tell a racist person from a not racist person until they, well, did something racist. Sure, there were hints and clues, things he could pick up on and was pretty good at spotting. But every now and then, he'd be completely blindsided by someone.

Once, it was another ranch worker who he enjoyed being partnered with for heavy work. The man had gotten mad at him after losing too many hands during an after-work poker game and started using slurs. Once, it was an owner's daughter who made a pass at him. And after he politely rejected her, suddenly her boyfriend was coming at him with fists. Another time everything was going perfectly, until a sweet old lady from the church came to visit and something 'mysteriously' went missing from her purse. That in and of itself wouldn't have been so bad, except she immediately accused Mick of being the one who robbed her —despite the fact that he'd been out working the entire time.

Obviously not the worst things in the world, but still something Mick would prefer not to deal with if he could help it. And again, there were so many more amazing stories than awful ones, but boy, did the bad ones have a way of sticking around the mind.

"But they are mighty generous, it seems," he said to Othello, who couldn't give two carrots about money, benefits or time off. "I've been paid less by bigger setups."

That was certainly the truth. He'd been particularly shocked by Cassidy's offer, although he was pretty sure he'd done an alright job of hiding it. But that kind of pay was going to put him well ahead and build his nest egg right up. He could travel for as long as he liked, and maybe the itch he felt to constantly move around would ease a little.

"What do you think, Othello? They're giving us free range all over this place, basically. You'll have lots of room and maybe a couple of pretty lady horses to look at."

Othello made a sound like he very much enjoyed that idea, which had Mick chuckling again. He felt like he really hadn't had time to hang out with his best friend in over a week, and it was nice to just have a quiet time together while not being cramped in his little trailer.

"Alright, I think you've had enough brushing. Let me get some of that feed they offered us."

Mick had his own supply, he had to for traveling, but that Cassidy had been very insistent he use theirs while he was at the ranch and save his for later. She was an interesting one, that was for sure.

When she'd first spotted him in the door, he was sure she was mighty peeved. But it was after she drew a blanket up to her neck and a flush colored those tanned cheeks of hers that he realized she was just embarrassed. And that was good. For him, at least. Her being bashful that she wasn't presentable when meeting him usually implied that she thought that he was her equal and worth impressing. Of course, there were some vain people who felt that way about anyone, but he got the feeling that Cassidy wasn't like that.

She *did* seem anxious, however. Prideful. Maybe even resentful of her situation. Not that Mick could blame her. He knew what it was like when he wanted to do one thing, but his body forced him to do another. It wasn't a good feeling.

But there had been a couple of times she'd smiled, especially at the end there, where he could see who she might have been before her accident. She had an amazing face, that Cassidy, and it was emphasized by the short, pixie cut she sported. Funny, she and Clara were both lookers, but while Clara was all classic beauty and softness, Cassidy was more... rough?

No. That wasn't the right word. But her features were sharper. More angular, with a sharp chin and even sharper cheekbones. He wondered if there was native blood in their family but figured he couldn't rightly ask. They had some of those features, though.

Mick was pulled from his musings by Othello's snout wuffling hot air into his grown-out hair.

"Yeah, yeah. I know it's longer than it used to be. Now that we're settled, I'll probably fade it back out tonight. New beginnings deserve some polished edges, right, my guy?"

Othello snorted, shaking his head again, but somehow even more dramatically.

"Right, right. Wrong guy to speak to about having short hair. Not all of us want to deal with the maintenance of having long hair. Besides, we both know that you'd chew on any locks or twists that I got done."

The horse didn't even bother to deny it, the scoundrel. Just made a sighing noise and looked to the empty trough. That was Othello, through and through, and Mick's heart warmed from it. He would be alright, as long as he had his right-hand man—er, *horse*—always by his side.

And who knew, maybe the Millers would want to breed the big guy with some of their own stock. They'd mentioned they'd cut down on their horses, but part of ranch life was being flexible to opportunities when they were presented. Mick could certainly use the money that would come from a siring fee.

It wasn't a permanent home, that was for sure, but it was someplace nice to stay for three to six months. Maybe, if he did well enough, he could buy a nicer camper. Maybe even get a house of his own.

Of course, in order to get a house of his own, he'd have to find a place he actually wanted to build a home. And that was proving much harder than he ever thought.

5

Cassidy

"First, I stop by Charity's workshop and make sure that all of her cordless tools are charged or in their charging docks. It may seem silly, but I can't tell you how many times she'd haul all her stuff to somewhere on the ranch to fix somethin' only to find that was all the batteries were dead."

"That's surely considerate of you, miss."

Cass smiled crookedly at his comment. Maybe from others it would sound patronizing, but from Mick's low, rarely used voice, it simply sounded like he was stating a fact. "I was serious about being her second-in-command. I don't have the eye for detail she does, and I can't just put things together like she does, but I'm real good at making her job easier."

"Lot of people wish they had someone like that."

Perhaps she shouldn't have, but Cass felt a flicker of pride.

He got it. Then again, she wasn't sure if anything was ever able to ruffle that mysterious demeanor of his.

After all, it was his first day on the job. He was cool as a cucumber having her right there with him, showing him her chores step-by-step. She could have written out a list, or maybe even sent Clara, but she didn't. She wanted to be there, because being there made it seem almost like she was actually working.

If he was surprised by her being so hands-on, he didn't say anything. And if he thought her walking him through it made her feel less useless, well he didn't say anything about that either.

Actually, he just didn't say much in general. When he did, she was anxiously clinging to each word.

Of course, with that much time spent with him quietly completing tasks exactly as she asked him to do, it gave Cass's mind plenty of time to make up wild and elaborate stories about him and how he got there. After all, she knew he started in some sort of city in the east—she guessed New York City— and ended up on her little homestead, so that was quite a gap to fill.

And strangely enough, she was having a great time mentally inserting different scenarios, all of them entirely too dramatic. It was like her own personal soap opera, with the handsome lead right in front of her.

"Now that we've got that out of the way, we've got some hay to cut and then some thorns that cropped up way over on the south side we have to clear."

"Of course, miss. Lead the way."

That was another thing; he never *once* argued with her. Even if her methods were peculiar, even if she was needlessly particular, he just nodded and did what she asked. And, on the rare moment he asked a question, it was only to clarify something he didn't understand. It wasn't what Cass was expecting, considering that she was both a woman and young. Every now and then, when they'd hired an expert or temporary contractor to come help them with a project, the man who inevitably arrived would usually treat Charity or Cass like they didn't know what they were doing. Eventually, they would relent, but Cass had been prepared to go through that same process with Mick.

Except, apparently, she didn't need to.

When they reached the hay that needed to be cut, Mick finally spoke again. "Are you going to stick around while I do this, or are you going to come back later?"

"I figure it takes me so long to get to the house and back that I might as well stay here."

"Alright then."

And without any more discussion, he got to work, taking the tools out of the truck without so much as a bat of his eye. Cass figured that it would be kind of weird to just stare at him, so she pulled her notebook out and started to write out different lists.

One of them was all the chores she wanted to show Mick. Another was the new plants she wanted to try in Dad's garden the next spring. And even more were different banner ideas for their stand at the yearly festival. Another was just random possible gift ideas for birthdays in the coming year, anything to keep her both occupied and productive.

But even as she tried not to stare, she still found her eyes sliding to Mick, watching the muscles of his wiry frame bunch and ripple as he went about cutting the hay. There was a rhythm to how he moved, and it fascinated her.

Goodness, she was acting like she'd never seen a well-built man before in her life, which obviously wasn't the case. After all, Alejandro was a delicious slice of man-cake by all rights, but from the moment she saw him, she *knew* he'd be perfect for Charity.

And she was right, for all intents and purposes. Charity and Alejandro were going strong, with little Savannah becoming not so little incredibly fast.

Before she knew it, her phone's alarm was going off. Already, it was time to head to the house for lunch and all the pills she needed to take. Great.

"Hey, Mick. It looks like it's lunchtime."

"Alright, do you need me to drive you back, miss?"

"Well, I'd assume you'd need to drive yourself back at least." He just blinked at her. That was when Cass realized that she'd forgotten to tell him just how much Clara cooked and that he was more than welcome to help himself.

After all, between her and Papa, there were almost always leftovers, and on the incredibly off chance there weren't, there were plenty of supplies to make lunch.

Cass spoke up to fix the situation. "You don't *have* to eat with us, but I guess I kind of expected it."

There was the slightest widening of his eyes. Cass felt a surge of pride that she was already starting to decode his expressions.

"You did?" he asked.

"Yeah, is that weird? It's just, we have so much food and Clara loves feeding people... and it's not like you can stop working in the middle of day to make yourself a whole meal, so, I dunno, it just made sense."

"I...see."

"Again, you don't have to, if you don't want to."

"I'm game to try anything once. I'm sure my blood sugar will thank you anyway."

She may have babbled one or two things that didn't make a ton of sense, but he didn't point any of it out as she got into the truck. He placed her chair in the back for her, folding it up without missing a beat.

The trip was short and, just as she suspected, Clara had grilled Rueben-like things waiting for them and Charity. They all sat around the living room and Mick was incredibly polite, bordering on stiff.

"If you don't like it, don't worry. I have plenty of other things I can whip you up in just a second. Never an empty pantry around here, you know," Clara said with a smile.

"I'm fine, thank you."

"So, Mick, my sister said she met you at the grocery store?" That was Charity's attempt at getting him to talk more, but he only nodded at that.

Cass was well aware of her siblings exchanged glances, which only grew in frequency as Charlie popped in.

"Hey, I was just swinging by to say hi and—oh, who is this?"

"Charlie!" Clara said, already up and handing their brother a packed lunch. "This is our new worker, Mick. Mick, this is Charlie. He's the middle child and just about everything you'd expect from that."

"Hey, I take offense to that," her brother said with a crooked grin. "And good to see you took my advice, sis."

That last part was directed at her, but Cass was hardly listening. She was so *exhausted* suddenly and she hadn't even taken her medicine yet. Suddenly, even keeping her eyelids up was practically impossible, making her head droop towards the table.

"Miss, are you feeling alright?"

Hazily, she tilted her head up just enough to see Mick

looking at her with concern from across the wooden surface. "Yes. It's just I…" She couldn't think, her mind going kind of sideways and sinking into the mud. She needed to do so much more on his first day, but she couldn't get her body or brain to respond at anything other than a glacial pace.

"Hey, Cass, I'm guessing you got a list for all you wanted your new hire to do?" Charlie asked casually. That was one thing she loved about her brother; he was so matter-of-fact about most things.

"In my bag."

"Alright, how about me n' the new guy just go handle that after lunch while you go take a nap?"

"But…"

"I don't mind, miss," Mick added on just as coolly.

It was embarrassing to need a nap as a grown woman, to the point where she was about to faceplant on the table, but it wasn't like she could pretend otherwise. She felt like she had just downed a whole bottle of sleeping pills. "Oh… okay."

Somehow, she made it through the rest of the meal, although it turned into a blurry mess. When it was over, Charlie gave her a kiss on the cheek while Mick tipped his head in respect, then Clara was rolling her over to the elevator. It made her cheeks burn to need to be so… so… so attended to, but she was too tired to do anything about it.

She wished it didn't have to be that way, but as long as she actually hung back and let Mick do what he needed, there was no reason she wouldn't be back up on her feet in the next quarter.

6

Mick

"Okay, so the list here mentions something about some brambles overgrown. We should head there."

"Are there any tools we could bring with us? Shovels? Picks?"

"Nah, there are big ol' sheers in the back. Should be enough. If not, I'll just light 'em up or somethin'."

Mick didn't say anything else as he and the brother drove to where the overgrowth was, but he kept getting the feeling that Cassidy would prefer if they were more thorough about it. Neither pruning back nor burning seemed like very good ideas.

Naturally, he didn't mention that, and just mechanically went through what he needed to do. But that was mostly because his mind kept going back to Cassidy and the strange mishmash of contradictions that she was.

At first, when she'd shown up on his first day to tell him everything to do and how, he thought that her need for control and micromanaging were going to be a huge source of tension. But as the day went by... well, he kind of got it.

It was clear that the woman took great pride in her home and their ranch and felt some type of way about not being able to take care of it. Mick was less an employee and more like her surrogate hands. That had helped settle him, but it hadn't been until she asked him to lunch that he began to see her in a different light. He'd been uncertain about it, sure, but then how slumped and defeated her shoulders had been made him feel like he'd seen a very secret, vulnerable part of her that most people weren't allowed to see.

And it was in his head, turning those moments over and over. How her head had hung slowly, her thick lashes batting sluggishly as she fought to keep her eyes open. How she'd struggle to answer her siblings. Whatever accident she'd had had clearly done a number on her.

The hours passed quickly and before he knew it, he was being dismissed with a grin by the brother. He was a tall, well-built fellow with what Mick was quickly realizing was the Miller family bone structure. He was pleasant enough, but clearly young and full of the energy that came with still being in his early twenties. With thirty marching ever closer to Mick, he'd never quite felt his age as much as he had recently.

"If this is what I'm like at twenty-eight, I'd hate to see how I get by forty-eight," he remarked to himself with a chuckle as he readied Othello up for a nice, easy ride. "If the world's still around, that is."

That was one of the reasons that, even as a kid, he'd wanted to get out of the city. Out of *all* cities. Something about the countryside gave him a respite from all of that. Sure, he never forgot about overcrowding of low-income areas. How even the most promising politicians would eventually be bought out, or just how obsessed some people were with money. Being out in the quiet with Othello... well, it helped.

Still, even at a calming trot, he couldn't help but wonder exactly who the Millers were—strange breed that they clearly were. Their mansion was *huge*, far larger than anything else he'd seen with its same aesthetic, and Cassidy hadn't even batted an eye at his pay.

Huh.

They had to be old money, but they didn't really act like old money. He hopped on the internet once he was showered and in his lounging clothes in his RV.

It didn't turn out to be hard to find them at all. He didn't even finish typing in the name fully before it was auto-filled and a whole *bunch* of information came up. What was he even getting into?

"I guess there's only one way to find out..."

It wasn't exactly a quick affair, and before he knew it, hours had already passed. *Wow*, there was a lot to the Millers. They were indeed from old money. Old, *old* money that, thankfully, wasn't derived from slavery or plantations. They had several ranches across the western half of the continent, including a megacorp in Texas and a smaller, more grassroots one higher north.

He found something about a wife, an internet personality, an animal shelter, a scholarship fund and a whole bunch of other articles ranging from incriminating diatribes about underpaid employees and exploitive practices, to applauding a new community center.

And then, right at the end, he found a long article written about the memorial wing built at the local school about none other than the matriarch of the small ranch he was on. She'd passed over a decade earlier, so Cassidy must have been young when she'd lost her mother.

That... explained some things. Her fierce independence and clear resentment for her wheelchair. Also, how much they loved the ranch. Mick was sure that there were reminders of her mother all over the place, in the walls of their mansion, in the animals and gardens. He never knew his parents enough to have any of that, but still... he could sympathize.

"Well, I think I've done enough snooping for the night," he murmured to himself, wiping a hand over his face. He almost felt nosey, like he'd snooped through Cassidy's personal belongings. He'd read a lot of drama—especially with the Texan part of the family. While he was sure that there was a lot of backstory that wasn't available on the world wide web, it didn't always cast the family in a positive light.

Sighing to himself, Mick closed his laptop and went about his nightly routine. Although he was plenty tired from his first real active day in weeks, he found sleep eluding him, the Millers and Cassidy filling his thoughts.

They were interesting folks, that was for certain, but he knew better than to get too close or too involved. Especially since he would probably be gone in three months. They would be a happy chapter in his life, but only a chapter.

If only the image of Cassidy being wheeled to that special elevator of hers, a miserable expression on her face, would get out of his head.

"Do me a favor and don't try to play hard to get with the family here, okay? We don't need to make waves."

Othello let out a wuff of a sound as they walked along, Mick atop his back in the afternoon sun. He'd finished up everything with Charlie more quickly than he'd expected, and it was the perfect time to take a ride on his mount. In a few weeks, it would be way too hot to go out any time before four, so he wanted to enjoy it while it lasted.

Maybe it was biased of him, but he'd half-expected Charlie to stand around and do nothing, as most rich young sons tended to do in his experience. But Charlie seemed just as happy to work as his sisters, even if he did get distracted more often.

It'd only been a single day, but already the Millers were quite different than what he expected. Were they just on their best behavior, or were they just one of the few that tipped stereotypes about the well-off on their heads?

He supposed he would just have to wait and see. It wasn't like he was big on planning anyway, preferring to roll with the punches and have the flexibility to go where he wanted to go and do what he wanted. Well, *generally* do what he wanted. He still had to work to make ends meet, but it helped that he genuinely enjoyed ranch and farm life.

"Hey, Othello?" he murmured, feeling a familiar sort of itch work its way up his spine. It was the same one that always had him pulling up his roots and moving along every six months or so, the urge to go, go, *go* if only to know that he was going somewhere.

His horse let out a questioning snort, no doubt recognizing Mick's particular tone. They practically had their own language, the two of them, one born from years of only having each other.

"Why don't you go ahead and run now."

He didn't have to ask twice. While Othello preferred to

strut and prance, he had a streak of fire in him that a lot of draft horses didn't. He took off, his hooves thundering across the grass, and Mick rode right along with him.

Wind in his hair, sun on his shoulders, it was everything he could have hoped for. That strange pull in him faded and for a moment, he could just *be*. Him, his horse, and his brand-new gig. Mick would enjoy it as long as he could, because it was only a matter of time before it went away and it would be time for him to go.

7

Cassidy

"Come on now, just one more lift with your leg and then we'll call it a day," Alejandro said, his strong arms resting just under her shaking calf.

"I can't," Cass panted, closing her eyes against the sweat rolling down her face, too wiped to even raise a hand to wipe the liquid away. "I *can't.*"

"You can, Cass. You've handled everything else I've handed to you and this is much the same. Just *one* more lift. I promise you can do it."

She was wrung out. So wrung out, her body emptied like a fuel barrel that had been drained to dryness. She'd been chewed up, scraped raw, and otherwise completely wrung out. Hadn't she earned a little rest?

"I think you're vastly overestimating my ability," she gasped.

"I haven't yet, have I? Trust me, Cass, I know you can do this."

Cass wanted to argue with him, to snap at him and tell him just because he had a fancy degree that didn't mean he knew everything about everyone, but she bit that urge back. That was just her anger talking, and she was trying not to indulge in that particular outlet. After all, her family and doctor were her biggest sources of support and they didn't deserve to be snapped at relentlessly.

Groaning, she put her everything into lifting her extended leg just a few inches off the PT bed that she was on. It was just a couple of inches. What was a couple of inches compared to everything else?

A lot, apparently, because it took every ounce of energy she had left to lift her leg that tiny bit and then set it back down.

If she wasn't lying down, she most certainly would have collapsed, her body essentially reduced to putty.

"Good job, Cass, good job. Now, how about I put the e-stim pads on while you cool down. Then we'll have you ready for when Charity comes around."

Cass went to nod, but her head wouldn't even move, her body protesting at anything even remotely related to any sort of locomotion. "Okay."

"You want me to get you some water too?"

"Maybe in a minute."

"Alright then. You still have that list of the new vitamin regiment I want you to try, right?"

"I got it. Don't worry."

Cass liked food as much as the next person, maybe even more, but between her medicine and how much she needed to sleep, her appetite had taken a big ol' dive. She'd never had a problem with staying nourished before the accident, but protein, iron, and calcium had been a real struggle ever since she was allowed to eat on her own.

So, vitamins it was. And Alejandro didn't have her on just what she was missing, but also probiotics to help her gut since some of her meds kind of gummed her already struggling digestive system up. Also, vitamin E eight hours before to make sure she could absorb the iron... It was a long, complicated list with specific times. She could eat some with food, some without food, some right when she woke up and others right as she went to bed. The regimen was enough to make her eyes cross, and she wasn't exactly looking forward to learning a whole new combination.

But it was what it was, and if she wanted to get better, then she needed to suck it up and do it. And she *did* want to get better. Sure, having the new ranch hand around certainly helped and she could kind of vicariously live through him, but he was just a temporary stop-gap so she wouldn't feel so guilty all the time for her siblings having to make up for everything she couldn't do.

She was quiet as Alejandro placed the familiar e-stim pads on her, and their mild buzz as they did their thing was kind of soothing. Before she knew it, her doctor was gently shaking her awake, telling her that Charity had arrived to pick her up.

Back when she'd first started her training with Alejandro, she'd been embarrassed with how he had to help her up and blot her forehead. But after the months they'd spent together, she'd gotten used to it.

Pesky thing, that pride. Always making things more difficult than they needed to be.

"Hello there, Charity," he said warmly as soon as she wheeled Cass out into the reception area.

At least that helped her cheer up. After everything her

sister Charity had been through, Cass loved that she'd found someone wonderful in Alejandro. Sometimes the brightest part of her day was seeing the two interact. Maybe it was sappy, but it gave her hope for the future.

Because, at the moment, her future mostly consisted of a whole lot of pain.

"Hey there, Alejandro. Savannah's in the car. Do you want to say hi?"

"Nah, I'll see her at dinner. You wanted me at your place by seven, correct?"

"That's the deal," Charity said, grinning in a way that Cass hadn't seen in years. It was almost like that awful ex of hers had never gotten a hold of her to break her heart so thoroughly. "Don't be late."

"I'll try my hardest." He gave her a quick kiss on the cheek, then Charity was wheeling Cass out.

"Do you want to stop for some ice cream?" Charity asked once Cass was safely in the truck. Even with her mini-nap inside, it'd taken considerable effort and a strong boost from her sister to get Cass inside.

"Honestly? I don't even think I could hold a cone long enough to actually enjoy it. Raincheck?"

Cass didn't miss the sadness in her sister's eyes. And Cass knew it had nothing to do with the ice cream. She was just mourning who Cass used to be, back before almost everything had been ripped away from her.

Don't be bitter, don't be bitter.

What was that her therapist had said? Bitterness was poison to growth? Well, sometimes Cassidy felt so full of bitterness that she was practically toxic. She tried to be pleasant, she tried not to take out her anger on everyone around her, but sometimes everything just seemed so *unfair*.

The conversation pretty much stalled out after that, and Charity wheeled her into the house in silence.

"Did you want to hang out down here or go up to your room?"

"Room, please. I want to rest. Then I'm going to shower off all this sweat."

"Sounds like a good plan. Is your shower stool in the bathroom still?"

"I don't know where else it would be. It's not like I take that thing around the house with me."

"Right, of course. I just wanted to make sure." She let out a sigh. "I'm mothering again, aren't I?"

"Only barely. But that's okay; it's been a long day."

Charity smiled at that, although it was small, and wheeled Cass to her personal wheelchair lift. Not too much later, she was slipping into bed and into a deep sleep.

IF CASS HAD HER WAY, she might have slept for a year or two. But as it were, Clara was waking her up *far* too soon.

"Ten more minutes," Cass groaned, rolling over and trying to cover her head with a pillow. She used to be such an early riser, but that skill had gone out the window along with her ability to function as an adult.

"Cass, it's time for dinner. I made something that would be easy on your stomach. Charity said you were pretty wiped out by your physical therapy."

Cass just groaned in response. She didn't want to eat. She didn't even really want to exist, for the most part.

"Sis, you need to take your vitamins. Just have a few bites of food, take your meds and your vitamins, and then you can sleep again."

She just wanted to *sleep!* Was that too much to ask? She was just so tired, and the fact that Clara was trying to tell her what to do like she was some teenager made her temper spike. "Could you just leave me alone?" Cass snapped, throwing her pillow across the room.

"Cass!"

Oh.

Well, she regretted that already.

"I'm sorry," Cass groaned, coming back to herself. "I... I didn't mean to. Are you okay?" She opened her eyes fully to seeing Clara standing in her doorway in one of her retro dresses, holding the pillow that she'd tossed.

"I'm fine. It was just a pillow. Are you okay? You're normally not so hard to wake up."

Cass took a deep breath, trying to fight off the shame that was coursing through her. Clara was the nicest of all their siblings, only wanting to help and take care of the animals. She didn't deserve to have things chucked at her. Even if it was a pillow.

"I guess I've had a rough day."

"I understand. Remember when I decked Charlie right in the face once when he tried to wake me up?"

"How could I forget; he tells that story every single birthday of yours."

"Well, that's what he gets for trying to wake me up early after I'd taken a melatonin."

Clara really was too kind. She should have been angry or at least reprimanded Cass, but instead she was joking and moving the subject right along. Cass truly didn't deserve her family.

"But anyway, do you want some help getting into your chair? I have everything all set out for you, so you don't have to be out long."

Cass was half-tempted to ask for whatever meal Clara had made to be delivered to her room, but one of her personal rules was that she no longer ate where she slept. Back when she had first returned from the hospital, she'd been stuck in her room for several weeks, only able to sit up as she ate, and she never wanted to go back to that again.

"Thank you. I could use some help."

Clara nodded, setting the pillow to the side, and that was that. Soon after, Cass was downstairs, drinking some thick potato soup with an only mildly shaking hand.

She did have a special spoon that Papa had bought her for when she had first come home. It had some sort of special technology in it that stabilized it from hand tremors. It was meant for people with disabilities to make them more self-sufficient, but Cass hated using it.

It was silly, she knew that, but she couldn't help it. She didn't want to be an invalid to the point of needing special eating utensils. She'd been a *ranch hand* before. She could repair fences, rope a cow, and harvest crops with the best of them. To be reduced to needing a special spoon simply for soup?

Her pride could only take so much.

So yeah, maybe she'd splashed a little on her front. That was fine; she was wearing sweaty PT clothes and hadn't had a chance to shower anyway. The point was, she got her medicine in her, her vitamins, *and* her food. Not bad for every single limb screaming at her to be in bed.

She was just about finished when Papa came in from his office, whistling to himself. She couldn't help but grin at him, her mood always improving whenever she saw his smiling face.

She had no idea how Papa managed to be so positive. She remembered how devastated he'd been when Mama had passed. How he'd cried every morning as he watched the sun rise, her empty coffee cup beside him as he sat on the front porch, and he'd retire early every night to sit in the quiet of his room. It had taken him a long while to recover, so Cass was never going to take having him around for granted.

Er... at least she tried not to.

But still, it had been nearly two decades since they'd gone from one parent to two, and she couldn't help but feel like there was still an underlying sense of melancholy to their patriarch. Sure, he smiled, he sang, he whistled, but there was just... something that seemed to hover over him sometimes, like a gloomy sort of shadow that was only visible when the light hit it just right.

Cass almost wished that he would find someone, maybe a nice older church lady who loved gardening as much as he did. But he expressed absolutely zero desire for any of that. Huh. Cass had done a pretty good job changing Charity's mind. Maybe she could do the same for her father?"

He spoke first. "Hey there, Sundance. You free to help me for a couple minutes?"

Help? Cass couldn't remember the last time she had actually been helpful to one of her family members. Perking up from her fatigue, she pushed her chair away from the table.

"Sure, what do you need?"

"I was doing some seed sorting for the fall garden, and I have most of it done, but I'm stuck on a few. Feel up for some autumn logistics?"

Cass had never been overly good at organization, but she

was so pumped at the idea of being useful she was nodding before he even finished his sentence.

"Sure, Papa. Sounds good to me."

"Great. I'll meet ch'a up there. I'm just going to get some of that hibiscus tea I brewed earlier."

"You and your teas," Cass remarked with a wry grin, heading towards her lift.

As it were, Papa didn't leave her waiting long, entering his office with a large glass of his iced tea. It was a pretty red, but Cass knew from experience that she wouldn't like it. Try as she might, tea just wasn't her thing.

"Alright, so where did you leave off?"

"Well, I was trying to plot out where I was going to put all our second wave of squash, but we have so many varieties that I'm running out of room."

Trust her father to have such a dilemma. The man was an ardent seed collector and compulsive seed saver, often leaving them with more than they could plant every year. Cass didn't mind, however, because he shared his seeds with plenty of people. And she figured out of all the things he could collect, something that grew into food wasn't really a problem.

"Do you have any favorites?"

"Oh, you know I do. We can't go without butternut, of course. And delicata. Patty pan too."

"Are those all summer or winter squash?"

"Mostly winter. I'm looking to have enough to last us all the way until the next harvest."

"Oh man, that's a lot. Are you giving them more than one bed?"

"I'm thinking about it. Maybe ripping out those tomatoes early that aren't really producing."

"Great idea, and are we amending the soil?"

"That we are."

It was a common misconception among new gardeners that summer squash was grown in the summer, and winter squash was grown when it was colder. That, however, wasn't true, and Papa had made sure to teach all of them back even when they were young little tykes. In fact, Summer and Winter squash could be grown side by side, because the real difference was just in how long they lasted.

Summer squash were meant to be eaten within the season, ergo, during the summer. Their rinds were thinner, and they didn't store as well. But *Winter* squash was meant to last for almost a year if it was cured properly, lasting all the way through the cold season until it was time to grow again. That was one of the reasons squash had been quite important to a lot of different cultures that had harsh winters.

"Okay, well we want to focus on winter squash then. Why don't you lay out everything you have and we'll compare grow times?"

Papa smiled fondly at her. "You're always the practical one. I knew you'd be great at this."

She flushed as he did what she asked, the conversation stilling naturally as he laid out his impressive collection. She was so intent on it that she wasn't prepared at all for when he spoke again.

"Why don't you go to church anymore, Cass?"

Well, that certainly hit her out of nowhere, and she blinked at him. "What?"

"Church. You used to go at least every other week, but you haven't gone in at least a couple of months. I miss you there. I always loved singing the harmonies with you over the hymns."

"That's kind of a loaded question, Papa."

"I know, but if you're willing to share, I'm willing to listen."

"Well..." Cass thought for a moment, her walls wanting to slam closed on the conversation. It was too close to talking about what happened to her, but she was so *tired* of all that. At least with the seeds she'd been able to forget how she was trapped in her chair, trapped in a body that suddenly couldn't do even half of the things she wanted it to. "I guess it's a couple of things."

Papa didn't say anything, seeming to know that she needed to parse out her words.

"First of all, they don't have a wheelchair ramp going up, so that makes it real difficult to get in. I know Charlie can carry me on his back, but..."

"That's humiliating?"

"Yeah. I'm a grown woman. I don't want to be carried on anybody's back."

"Right, I understand that." They were quiet for a minute before he spoke again. "Is that the only reason?"

He said it so softly she would have missed it in any other room, but they were so close together in the quiet that even a pin drop would have been thundering.

"I guess I'm angry."

"Angry at who?"

"You *know* who I mean, Papa."

"I believe I do, but I want to hear it from you."

Frustration lanced through her and Cass had to bite her tongue until her tone settled out. She didn't use to be so terse. "I'm mad at God, alright? I don't understand why he did this to me, and why the person who hit me got away with a broken leg while I almost died. I don't understand why he keeps throwing roadblock after roadblock at me. Did I do something wrong? Am I being punished? Did I think too many bad thoughts or tell too many white lies?" Cass realized that her voice was rising, and she took a steady breath. "I know being in church brings you comfort, but right now, it does the opposite for me."

Her father didn't answer right away, just looking at her with those intense and gray eyes of his. She'd been told hundreds of times that she'd inherited his eyes almost exactly, but Cass had never seen it.

"Alright."

"...alright?" Cass questioned, not sure if she'd heard him correctly. "You're not trying to convince me otherwise?"

Gently, he wrapped an arm around her shoulder, leaning down so they were face to face. "Sundance, your walk with God is your own, and I'd be about as wrong as I could be if I tried to force you onto mine. If you and the big guy need time to work things out, then you take all the time you need."

"Really?"

He shrugged. "You can talk to God anywhere. And it sounds to me like the two of you have a lot of difficult conversations ahead of you. So just promise me you will try to work it out."

Cass felt her eyes begin to sting, a telltale sign that she could potentially tip over right into crying.

"Thank you, Papa. I'll try."

"Sundance, I'm here for you in whatever you need, even if that's just being quiet and letting you figure everything out."

"That means a lot, Papa. It really does."

"I'm glad, sweetheart. Just remember, although I'm happy to let you do whatever you need to do on your own, you're never completely alone. Not in this family."

That soothed her, coating her heart in a syrupy sort of warmth. "I won't forget, I promise."

"That's my girl."

8

Cassidy

"Hey, Cass?" Clara said, sitting across from Cass in the living room with an intense expression on her face.

"What's up?"

"I need to talk to you, but I don't want you to be angry with me."

Well that was certainly one way to start a conversation. "Angry with you? Why would I be angry with you?"

She chewed her lip a moment, a habit that was uniquely Clara. She always liked to do right by people and hated upsetting anyone. Sometimes Cass worried about people taking advantage of it, but at least her sister was an excellent judge of character.

"Okay, so, well... I noticed you haven't been going to church at all, and I know you used to be pretty into the worship team, so I got to thinking."

Geez, was it really so noticeable that she wasn't going to church anymore? It wasn't like she was a vital part of the congregation or anything.

"Uh-huh?"

"I was thinking, and I realized they don't have any ramps and there are like seven steps to get into the front door. I feel bad that I'd forgotten how Charlie had to haul you up there on his back."

"Yeah, a pretty inconvenient thing when I was wearing a skirt."

"Right! Exactly! So, while I was thinking, I also realized that there were plenty of older parishioners who are having issues getting around too, and that number is only going to grow as people age."

"You have a point. The place needs more than just a handicapped stall in one of their bathrooms."

Although it wasn't a fancy mega-church like the one they used to go to, it wasn't a Podunk single room chapel either. No, her family had personally poured plenty of money into that place along with the other farm families in the area.

"That's exactly what I thought!" Clara clapped her hands together, her excitement growing quickly. It was funny how her middle sister was just one contradiction on top of the other, and yet it made sense for her. "So anyway, I went to the church, and I got to talking to the board about accessibility. Mind you, I was willing to sponsor expanding the bathrooms, adding a wheelchair ramp, and including some wider pews, but then Marybeth—you remember Marybeth, right?"

"I do."

"Great! Well Marybeth suggested we do a fundraiser and I could help run it along with my donation if I wanted."

Cass swallowed hard, feeling that familiar prickle in her throat. Goodness, since when had she turned into such a crybaby?

"You did that for me?"

"Well, yes. But also, no. I was inspired by you, but I realized I wanted to help a bunch of people in our community."

"That's great, Clara."

"I'm glad you think so. Because, well, the reason I'm here is because I need your help."

Oh? Was her whole family conspiring to try to give her a purpose or had her luck just suddenly turned around? That latter one seemed doubtful.

"I was going to keep this a secret from you then surprise you day-of, but something's come up and I don't have quite the free time I thought I would. Besides, I realized that it was strange to have all able-bodied people deciding how to make the church more friendly to the differently abled."

"What's come up?"

Not that Clara wasn't ambitious, but she was kind of a homebody. She had the chickens, Papa's garden, her chores, cooking and then the church. That, along with makeup and fashion, pretty much encompassed her entire day-to-day life.

"Well, do you remember that gentleman who was struck by lightning during the same storm you were hurt in?"

Cass nodded. "I do. The town newspaper had a whole lot of content for a good month there."

"Well, he's had a setback with things, and I've decided to basically help run his little homestead while his skin grafts are still setting and while he's dealing with everything else."

"Didn't you say something about him not liking you?"

But Clara just shrugged. "I don't see how that matters."

"You don—" Cass shook her head. "Only you, Clara."

But her younger sister just kept right on going. "So, is that something you would be interested in? I understand if you aren't, and I can definitely find someone else if you're already pretty booked, but I would really love to do this with you! We haven't done any sort of project together since we built the pergola in Papa's garden."

Cass thought for a long moment, wondering if Clara and Papa had had a talk behind her back. But it didn't seem likely, especially considering that lying wasn't really either of their schticks.

She didn't really want to be involved at the church at the moment. She had been serious when she'd told her dad that she was angry at life, God, and everything in general. She needed time to work on that and figure out what to do with all the vitriol trapped in her broken body.

But... the idea of helping others like her was definitely appealing. Sure, she didn't want to go to church, but she was sure Miss Betty did, and her hip was going out last Cass knew. And then there was Mr. Paul, a wonderful man who was developing some pretty awful arthritis that made bending his knees almost impossible. The idea of making them happy or relieving their struggle warmed her, and she already felt less useless.

"Alright. I'll help."

Clara clapped her hands again, her eyes going wide. "You will!? Thank you, thank you, thank you, Cass! I'm so excited! Okay, I have a whole bunch of info I need to give to you. And I'd like us to talk to the board. When would work best for you?"

"I'll look at my schedule once I'm upstairs; I left my phone in the bathroom."

"Okay. That makes sense. It gives me time to make a few calls." She stood, her mint-colored wedges clicking across the floor.

"Oh, and Clara?"

"Yes, love?"

"Whatever you're donating, I want to match it."

Cass didn't need to turn around to hear the smile on her sister's face. "You've got it.

9
———

Mick

*D*espite the bumps he'd expected, it was surprisingly easy to settle into a rhythm on the ranch. Cassidy worked with him sometimes, and sometimes she didn't. Occasionally her sister Charity would accompany her, or her brother Charlie, but mostly it was just them. The days began to blend one into the other with plenty of time for him and Othello to wear themselves out with riding, grazing or just messing about. No one believed him when he said that Othello liked frisbee, but it was one of the first things a younger Mick had taught the giant guy.

And the more he worked with Cassidy, the less she had to instruct him. It'd taken some adjustment, but after a week passed, he began to get her flow and how her mind worked. It was easy to anticipate what she wanted and how she would fix things. And if he also noticed how her lips would curl in surprised satisfaction whenever he anticipated her, well that was something he kept to himself.

Aside from all the stereotypical ranch hand chores he helped with, he also replaced the fencing around their father's garden with Charlie and the patriarch himself. At first Mick had been taken aback that it was 'Papa Miller' who was in charge of the garden, but then he remembered that one: there wasn't any gender requirement for loving to grow food, and two: Mrs. Miller was dead and the garden could be his strongest connection with her memory. Thankfully, he had the good sense not to say anything before his mind put two and two together, so he saved himself from accidentally mocking a widower.

But for the most part, he did try to keep to himself and let the summer pass quickly. Before he knew it, two months had passed, and they rolled right into the hottest parts of the year. He still ate lunch with the Millers every once in a while, but usually he tried to remember to pack everything he needed for his shift to keep him energized and healthy.

"Wait, what's going on here?"

Mick stopped in his tracks from where he'd been working to cut down an old tree for firewood, his eyes going over to one of the irrigation paths the Millers had dug out that led from a natural pond at the highest part of their property down to their goat pen and their grazing area. It normally flowed at a pretty consistent rate, but he could see that part of it was full nearly to the top and not going anywhere.

Setting his ax in the wagon he'd carted along with him, he jogged over only to find that a load of brambles combined with what looked like a coyote corpse and mud were blocking part of the pathway, causing a piece of tarp to catch on it and heavily stall the flow of water.

"*Ugh*, I'm surprised I didn't smell that from my camper."

He needed to clear it, obviously, but he was pretty sure that he couldn't just weaken the sides until the force of the water washed the rest away. Not unless he wanted the contaminated water to be washed down into the goat's main water supply. For the first time in weeks, he felt like he wasn't sure what Cassidy would do if she were in his boots.

Well, the best way to find out would be to ask.

Despite his usual attempts to give their rustic manor a wide berth, he figured it would be easy to go there, refill his water canteen while he was at it, and ask Cassidy if she already had a protocol in place or if she wanted to see the clogged area herself. And hey, if he got to linger in their exceptional air conditioning for a few extra minutes, well, that would just be a happy coincidence.

Making sure the axe was secure, he turned on the four-wheeler he'd hauled the small wagon with and headed back towards the manor. It didn't take him long to get there, but he was surprised to see all of the cars gone.

Huh, a busy day indeed.

"Miss?" he called with a knock, letting himself in. "I found something I need your advice on!"

There wasn't an answer at first, not by Cassidy, her sister Clara or anybody else for that matter. In fact, the house was strangely still, perhaps for the first time since he'd arrived. Although, again, he did try to make a point of avoiding the main house, so maybe it wasn't that unusual of an occurrence?

"Miss?"

Worry began to prickle along his spine, something about the warm, welcoming manor being so still setting him on edge. He walked further in, not wanting to trespass but definitely wanting to get his employer's attention.

"Miss, I need your advice. Are you awake?"

Another step in, and then another, and that was right about when he spotted a hand on the floor, fingers pale and curled.

"Cassidy!"

Running, he practically leaped over the couch to see Cassidy sprawled across the floor, one leg on the couch and another on their coffee table. There was a knocked over cup by her head and thankfully, judging from the size of the puddle around her, it hadn't been there overly long.

"Miss, are you alright!? Can you hear me?"

He rushed to her side, bending down to listen for breath. He felt it across his face instantly, warm and slightly damp, while her chest rose and fell at what he was pretty sure was a healthy rate.

Should he call 911? Clara? He wasn't certain. He hesitated, phone in his hand, but before he dialed, he saw Cassidy's eyelid flutter.

"*Hhhng?*"

"Miss! Are you alright?"

She blinked at him a few moments, looking around as if she was seeing the room for the first time. "Wha... what are you doing here?"

"I needed your advice and found you on the floor. Are you alright? Should I call your doctor for you?"

"What? No, no, I'm fine." She rubbed her head, and to his great surprise, let out a truly massive yawn.

"I found you unconscious on the ground. I don't think that quite goes under fine."

"Unconscious... what?" At that she seemed to come back to herself and *laughed*. Mick stared at her, confused. What exactly was so amusing? "I'm sorry, I really appreciate you, but I just took a nap on the couch and I must have rolled out."

Now it was Mick's turn to stare at her. "You... napped?"

"Yeah, I'm sorry. I know what this looks like. But I was so beat after physical therapy, combined with taking my meds knocked me right out. I... why am I wet?"

"You knocked over a cup when you rolled off the couch," Mick said, letting out a long breath. Alright, maybe she had a point. It was kind of funny. But it was hard for him to laugh along when he was still so full of adrenaline. He'd really thought she was *hurt*, and his body felt like it was still on high alert from it.

"Huh, wow. That's impressive. Even for me."

Mick took a deep breath, trying to collect his scattered thoughts. "Alright, let me at least get you off the floor and clean this up."

"What? Oh, you don't have to do that. I—"

"Ma'am, I realize you're probably perfectly cable of taking care of yourself, but it would help me get over the shock if you let me take care of things."

It was the sternest tone he'd ever used with her, and her eyes went wide. "Oh, I'm sorry. I didn't realize you were... I... that must have been a real shock to you. Of course, do whatever you need."

"I appreciate that, miss."

And he did, really. He hadn't known that seeing her sprawled out like that would feel like something out of his worst nightmare, but it absolutely did, and his heart was still thundering. It touched on an old fear in him, back when he'd been a preteen and his nana's health had been declining. Every time he'd come home, he'd been scared he'd find her body, or that she'd collapsed into some sort of diabetic coma in his absence.

"Here, let me give you a hand up."

He could have scooped her up, he was pretty sure, but he also wasn't foolish enough to think Cassidy would ever allow to be that coddled. So instead, he offered his outstretched palm and he was quite pleased when she took it.

Maybe it was because adrenaline was already pumping through him, maybe it was because he hadn't had physical contact with a human in weeks, but either way, he seemed hyper-aware of the texture of the skin across her palm and fingers.

Soft, surprisingly soft, and warm. Yet there were rough patches of callous exactly where his nana had them as well. Wheel chafing, if he remembered right.

"I'm sorry, you know," Cassidy said, drawing his attention back. "I didn't—"

Mick shook his head, letting go of her hand so he could pick up the cup and other scattered items. "You don't have anything to apologize for, miss. I'm just peculiar about these things."

She didn't say anything to that, just watching him and mussing her sleep-wild short hair. Was it strange that the sleepy-slow movement was almost... cute? He was fairly certain that Cassidy would sucker punch anyone who dared to call anything about her adorable.

He needed to stop trying to watch her out of his peripheral vision. She was fine, and he could calm down. She had just been sleeping and he'd come in at an unfortunate time.

Keeping a sigh to himself, Mick fetched paper towels from the kitchen to clean up the water, and when everything was pretty much back in place, he turned back to Cassidy.

She was still looking up at him, her eyes catching the sun just right to look like something out of a movie when they did that soft-focus thing with their starlets. Her gaze was intense, as he'd noticed with most of the other Millers, but how had he not noticed that one of them was half brown, the color ending in a jagged line of the honeyed color. Heterochromia? He'd heard of that before in passing, but he'd never seen a case of it up close and found himself staring right back.

"Thank you," Cassidy said finally, the column of her throat bobbing as she swallowed.

Mick's gaze followed that too before he realized that he needed to actually *speak*. Goodness, what about the hurt woman always made him forget what few social skills he had?

"No thanks needed. Just glad I was able to get you up before you got a horrible crick in your neck from the floor." But that didn't seem to be enough. Mick didn't want to go. He wanted to... to hover. To make sure she was alright. "Do you... need your pain medicine? Can I get you a snack? Do you need anything?"

At that her cheeks flushed ever so slightly and those lips of hers curled into one of the smiles he always liked.

"You know, you don't have to hover."

Mick just shrugged. "It's just, I'm reminded of taking care of my nana. Not that you're old or anything."

"You're full of surprises, aren't you, Mr..."

"Just call me Mick, please."

"Alright then. And you call me Cassidy. But, to answer your question, we do have a heating pad under the sink in the downstairs half-bath, and I wouldn't be offended at all if you grabbed it for me."

He hurried to do just that, but on his return, he didn't miss Cassidy's sharp wince as she tried to adjust herself on the couch. She was clearly hurting, and he had a feeling it wasn't *just* her physical therapy. Whatever accident she had been in was still very much affecting her acutely. Would... would another month really be enough time for her to heal and take over all the chores that Mick did? He doubted it.

"What about food? Shouldn't you get something in you? At least to get your blood sugar up?"

"I appreciate this all, Mick. But I'm fine. Really. If you plug the heating pad in, I'll be right as rain."

There was that pride again. But Mick knew how to deal with it. "I'm glad to hear that. But I was really overheating out there, so I was going to ask if you'd mind me taking a break in this AC?"

"Oh, of course! It was already blazing when I came home from therapy. I can't imagine how bad it is now. What is it... two o'clock?"

"Almost four, actually," Mick answered. "Mind if I grab myself a drink?"

"You know you're more than welcome."

"I suppose. What can I grab you while I'm up?"

Those intense, keen eyes of hers narrowed at him. She knew what he was up to, but thankfully, she didn't call him on it.

"You know what? I wouldn't mind some of the sweet tea from the pitcher in the fridge. And I think Clara was practicing making new, fancy tea sandwiches earlier. Why don't you grab those?"

"Practicing? She got something coming up?"

He asked the question while looking over his shoulder, so he wasn't rightly paying attention to his surroundings until he was standing nearly in the center of the room. He stood there a moment, shocked as he took it all in.

Wow, this is some high-tech stuff in here.

High-tech wasn't even the half of it. While the rest of the mansion he'd seen was all cottage-core, the kitchen was entirely chrome, it seemed, with fancy appliances and expensive pots hanging on a beautiful hanging display. The whole thing looked like it cost more than people could afford to spend on a whole house, and he couldn't help but whistle.

"The church is doing a big fundraiser to add a bunch of accessibility to both their property and the town hall. Clara's super excited about it and is going all out."

"Oh, is the charity for you?" Mick called back while he opened their truly massive fridge. Sure enough, there was a platter of different, cute sandwiches and a pitcher of sweet tea.

"What? No. We have far too much money to need *charity*."

Yikes, that was a soft spot. He kept that in mind for later.

"But... I probably inspired it. Apparently, folks in the congregation have been asking Clara why I don't come round anymore, and she told them they don't have a proper way for me to get into the building. I'm planning to donate about twenty grand myself."

Mick tried not to drop the pitcher. *Donating* twenty grand? While that certainly was a great gift, he couldn't imagine having twenty grand to just... just... give away.

Rich people were wild.

"That's awful generous of you."

"No, it's not particularly," Cassidy said, something strange to her tone. "Papa gave each of us access to our trust funds when we turned eighteen and lessons on how to invest along with how to pick financial advisors. All of us invested our money into enough stuff to pay ourselves a monthly salary for working on the ranch, and it's not a modest amount either. We have almost no expenses, and our ranch has its own expense account."

Mick didn't answer right away, digesting her words, but she kept on going.

"Sorry, I didn't mean to rant. I just don't think it's generous when I'm not really giving away anything I'll miss. I don't even think about money, ever really, so I guess I'm just... sensitive about being praised for it."

That was... that was surprisingly humble and understandable. Not that Mick thought that Cassidy wasn't a good person, but he wasn't used to people with wealth being so... practical about their situation.

"I get your meaning, miss," he assured her, bringing her the refreshments she'd requested before grabbing his own water bottle from the kitchen and sitting across from her.

"Do you? Because I'm not even sure I do."

He nodded, sipping at his own drink while he watched her slowly work on what he'd given her. His mind was whirring with questions, all of which were about one hundred percent none of his business.

"...do I have something on my face?"

"Pardon?"

Cassidy sent him that curled lip smile. "You're staring at me."

"Sorry, just thinking."

"What about?"

He wasn't used to people persisting after he was clearly being taciturn. "It's nothing."

"I'm old enough to know that it's never nothing, and the more you say it is, the more curious I'll become."

Mick withheld another sigh. That was why he didn't like

talking too much. It always made people ask questions, and the next thing he knew, he was saying something he shouldn't.

"It's, uh, it's inappropriate. Really, it's nothing."

"Inappropriate?" Her eyebrows shot up to her forehead and she looked down at her body as if she were trying to figure out what he meant. Once more, he'd chosen the wrong words.

"No, not like that. I just... I... your injuries. What happened to you? I keep wanting to ask, but I know that's your personal health information and if you wanted to share it, you would."

"Huh, normally people aren't so respectful of that boundary. But I guess, since it made the news around here, a lot of people feel that it's their business."

"I'm rightly sorry about that, miss. You don't have to tell me. I hope I didn't—"

"Call me Cassidy. And no, it's fine. It's fine, I want to tell you. As for what happened to me, I was hit by someone who shouldn't have been behind the wheel during one of the worst storms we'd had in a long time. I was lucky that I was on my phone with my sister at the time. Otherwise I don't know how long it would have taken them to find me."

A car accident made sense and was what he'd figured, but it was good to know for sure. But still, to have her in a wheelchair for so long after? It must have been an intense one.

"It was bad, like really bad. Front end crumpled in, my door inverted, dashboard practically crushing my chest."

Mick swallowed hard, able to picture it all so clearly. Sometimes, when he was on the highway and people brake-checked him, he'd have a horrible flash of a vision of the horrors that could happen from that if he wasn't paying attention.

But Cassidy hadn't had a vision. She'd *lived* it. Survived it.

...barely.

The thought of her being hurt, alone and in the cold horrified him. As did the thought that she had almost passed on. Was it abnormal to be so affected by something that was well in the past? Especially since it happened to someone he didn't know in the slightest.

"Yup. I'm real lucky, apparently, and I try to keep that in mind. But sometimes..."

He recognized both the frustration and the resentment that flicked across her features. "Sometimes it feels like you aren't. I get it."

"Oh? You been in a wreck before?"

"No, nothing like that. I just know what it's like when your body won't do what you want it to, and how frustrating it can be when everyone around you takes their health for granted."

"Huh. You know that?"

He knew she was fishing, but he felt his walls come back up. He was a private person, and even though he found himself strangely wrapped up in Cassidy's story, he wasn't quite ready to tell his own yet.

Was that unfair? Probably. It almost felt selfish. She trusted him with private, vulnerable information.

"It's fine. You don't have to tell—"

"I had heart surgery," he heard himself blurt out, cringing internally at his brusque tone.

"You what?"

"Heart surgery. When I was young. Almost didn't survive for a while there, but when I was better, my nana got me into this program that used pet and livestock therapy for inner-city kids. That's when I met my first horse."

"Really?" she smiled a soft grin at that. "That's amazing. I was wondering how you went from some big city to all the way out here."

He afforded her a small chuckle at that. "It's been a journey, that's for sure."

"Can I see it?"

Mick nearly choked on the water he'd just started to drink again.

"Oh, I'm sorry. Talk about inappropriate. I don't know why—"

"It's fine. I guess we've both asked one now, so we're square."

She let out a nervous sort of laugh and it made her cheeks flare brighter. "Hah, I guess."

"I would have to unbutton my shirt, if you wanted to see, that was."

"Oh, that's fine with me. Here! Let me show you one of mine!"

Before he could even think, she shifted onto one hip and pulled one of the legs of her loose basketball shorts *far* too high up her thigh. He knew his eyes went wide and that his gaze was locked on that peachy flesh, but before it could be creepy, he saw thick, pinky scars all across her leg with even more peeking out from below the hiked-up line of fabric.

"Gnarly, right? Maybe it's weird, but one of the things I noticed from a couple of the support meetings I went to was that survivors *love* showing off their scars. Except, ya know, burned folks. They uh, they very much do not like that."

"I can see why. It's a different sort of scar, isn't it?"

"Yeah, exactly. But like I said, you don't have to show me if you're not comfortable.

"No, it's alright. Fair is fair."

Cassidy beamed so brightly that he didn't realize that he'd crossed over to the couch until he was sitting down on it. Huh, that hadn't happened before. Should he be worried?

"Do you ever lie and tell people you got it in something cool, like a knife fight? Or like... I dunno, mountain lion attack?"

"No. I don't discuss it often, actually."

"Oh, so I'm special then?"

"I think you definitely are, Cassidy."

The pink on her cheeks grew more vivid and her gaze flicked to the floor. The momentary escape from her stare gave him a respite and he started in on his shirt. Despite his assurance, the hairs on the back of his neck definitely raised as he undid the top few buttons.

It was something simple. Perhaps even innocent. But with every button he could feel how the air grew more and more charged, like someone was pouring static into the room. Cassidy was staring at him again, her gaze practically boring through him as she leaned forward ever so slightly.

"Wow, it's thicker than I thought it would be. You said you got it as a kid?"

She leaned closer and Mick found that his tongue was suddenly heavy in his mouth. And *goodness*, he was thirsty. When was the last time he'd had any water?

"Does it tug at the living skin around it? Does it ache?"

"...sometimes."

He felt caught up in her, like the whole world was shrinking around them and pressing them closer and closer together.

"I've been wondering what these will feel and look like as I heal. It's been so long already, but really... I'm just getting started, I realize."

He nodded, wondering where all of his words went and why he wanted... he wanted...

Heart pounding, he could only stare as Cassidy reached

out, her comparatively pale fingers stretching towards him. Was she going to touch it? Why would she want to do that?

No answer came, but her fingers did indeed make contact, sending lightning coursing through his entire body. He wanted to press into those fingers, to have her trace all the skin around his scar and soothe it.

But that was completely and totally *wrong*.

Abruptly, he was standing up and Cassidy was staring at him, mouth hanging open in shock.

"I'm sorry! I shouldn't have—"

"If you'd excuse me," was all that Mick managed to get out before quickly striding through the door, Cassidy shouting apologies to him.

He didn't stop walking until he reached Othello and he hurriedly went through the motions of saddling him up. He just needed to ride somewhere, to get away from the mansion and Cassidy's incredible eyes.

But it wasn't until the draft horse was trotting along, the two of them heading for the edge of the property, that he realized he could still feel Cassidy's touch burning into his chest.

10

Cassidy

She probably shouldn't have touched Mick.

Well... she definitely shouldn't have touched Mick, and yet she most *definitely* had.

Cass stared out of the door where Mick had practically fled about half an hour earlier, hoping he'd come back but not quite willing to go after him. Especially considering how her muscles were still burning.

But even through all her embarrassment, she couldn't help but remember how that dark scar had felt under her fingertips in the fleeting seconds she'd been able to touch it. She didn't know *why* she did it, but...

There was just something about Mick. With his low voice and those onyx eyes of his, and then that story that made her feel so connected to him. With that bone structure and his skin that was so deeply black that it was almost blue...

Was... was she attracted to her employee?

There was probably no point in denying it or playing dumb, but Cass couldn't help but be shocked at herself. Sure, she'd been attracted to several people in her adult life—even dated a few—but after she saw the absolute trauma that Charity went through with her ex-husband, the whole thing had put her off of relationships of any kind.

Ugh. She needed to talk to someone. Clara maybe? She was always so good at listening.

"Clara! *Clara,* can you come down here?"

There was no answer for several moments, and Cass begrudgingly remembered that her sister had gone off to help some other invalid. It was hard not to resent whoever the guy was she'd taken off for. After all, Cass was *family.*

But she pushed those thoughts aside and decided she could always ask Charity, even if Cass always tried not to bug her elder sister unless it was dire.

"Alright. I just have to... get up, I guess."

It was easier said than done, but after about a half-hour of building herself up and stretching, Cass was able to get to her feet and hobble outside. She probably should grab her walker, but the thought of taking the extra steps to grab it from where she'd left it seemed like a terrible idea.

Thankfully, she made it outside and to the special moped that Charity had been working on for her ever since the holidays had passed. Six months of trial and error into making something just for her, and it was still... *glitchy.*

Nevertheless, Cass loved it and the fact that it allowed her to get over more of the ranch without worrying about tripping or tumbling over something. Granted, she tried to only use it when others were home and directly around the house in case something bad happened, but still, it was a welcome freedom.

Freedom that she needed. Ever since the accident, she'd had to live by so many rules and regulations that sometimes she felt like she was drowning.

Two months had been spent in the hospital, recovering enough just to get more surgeries to help her. Waiting for the swelling in her brain to go down. Then she'd gotten an infection that kept pushing her surgery date back. The final toll was three months, a quarter of a year, before they considered her healthy enough to go home.

She vaguely remembered reading that it would only take three to four months for a spine to heal after surgery, but apparently a spine being 'healed' didn't mean it was fully usable. There was the muscle atrophy she had to deal with, along with complications from being inactive for so long.

Her femur was supposed to take about half a year, but she was still in her long, long walking boot half the time. She usually had to sleep in it too just to ensure that she didn't jerk the wrong way in her sleep and jolt herself awake in terrible pain.

Then there was the traumatic head injury. That was the one with the most nebulous timeline of recovery. Some doctors told her that her progress was amazing, while others seemed concerned about issues she was still having. It hung like a thick cloud over her head, condemning her to her chair and everything else.

Sometimes, it made her feel more like a modern Frankenstein rather than a human woman.

"Ugh, get out of your head, Cassidy."

Despite the reprimand, she wasn't really able to extract herself from her thoughts until she spotted Charity in her garage, sketching out a new system for drip irrigation in Papa's garden.

"Hey, sis."

Charity started, her pencil flying as she whirled, only for her to heave a relieved sigh when she realized who it was.

"Geez, Cass, you startled me. What are you doing so far from home?"

Cass felt her temper flare up at that and had to beat it down. Her sister was just concerned for her, that was all. "I'm only at your garage, Char. It's not like I went to Narnia."

"Yeah, I know, but—never mind. Is something up?"

Cass thought about telling Charity what was going on, that she was attracted to their mysterious temporary employee, but her older sister was already going back to her sketchpad and dusting it off.

"No. Just wanted some air."

"Ah, I gotcha. I wish you would have called me to walk with you, but since you're here, do you want to help me out?"

"Sure. Sounds good to me."

Although Charity had trouble not mothering her, there wasn't an ounce of pity or saccharine sweetness to her request. It was just a matter of fact request for Cass's help. And that was something that Cass could absolutely get behind.

It was like old times, just her and her sis, Cass handing things to Charity or looking up specs on her phone. They fell into a familiar rhythm, one that Cass hadn't realized how much she'd missed. Just the two of them, making the ranch a better place for their whole family.

Eventually, she forgot about what was bothering her in the first place.

11

ick

"AM I BEING AN IDIOT? I'm being an idiot, aren't I?"

Othello picked up his foot and stamped it down lightly, shaking his head side to side. "No, I'm not calling *you* the dumb one. Just myself. Not everything is about you, you know."

The horse snorted as if he was challenging that very idea, and the sound made Mick feel better. At least he could always count on his horse to put a positive spin on things.

"I mean, all she did was touch me for like, less than a second. It really isn't a big deal."

Othello wuffled softly, his nose reaching towards Mick's satchel, no doubt hunting for apples.

"Hey, I didn't bring any this time. You're just going to have to do with my company, you big lug."

Othello responded by flicking his tail, his long, thick hair partially slapping against Mick's side. Right, well that was clearly what the horse thought about *that*.

But even with Othello's theatrics, Mick already felt more settled. He didn't have friends and wasn't really one for social media, so often the only one he really trusted with anything that was bothering him was his horse. Talking to the big guy was soothing in the way only a trusted companion could be.

"I'm just saying, I'm probably overreacting."

Yet, as much as he kept telling himself that, his feelings kept swirling up and down the scale at the short, less than a minute experience. If Mick closed his eyes, he could see the strangely intense look in Cassidy's eyes. He could feel that tingle that happened whenever anyone was *about* to touch someone but hadn't quite done so yet. He could smell the soft, subtle scent of her lotion and the fresh scent of her detergent.

So many details, so many impossible little factoids, and yet they were all encoded to his brain, playing over and over again in slow motion.

He shouldn't have been so affected. He had no logical reason to be so affected. And yet, as he talked to his closest friend, he couldn't deny that he was absolutely affected.

"Hey, you wanna go for a ride?"

Othello's head lifted at that, and he gave a few soft stomps, snorting quietly.

"Alright, I'll take that as a yes. Let's gear up."

Naturally, it didn't take long for them to be ready to go out and ride, Othello trotting out while neighing happily. He was always a pretty amiable guy, but his mood had definitely improved ever since they'd arrived. It was clear that all that time in the trailer was getting to him. Seeing the horse revel in the outdoors filled Mick with all the warm fuzzies he could want.

"Just so you know, it's going to get real hot soon. And we both know you hate being overheated, so be prepared for a lot of sunset and night rides."

Othello whinnied, tossing his head again while giving the closest he ever really got to a canter. Honestly, the big guy just seemed happy as long as he could spend a couple of hours outside. And he was definitely getting that and more considering that Charlie usually let him out into the horse pen with all of the Miller's mounts every single morning.

"Alright, well you're in charge for now, my friend. Take me wherever you want at whatever speed you want. Free ride, big guy."

It had taken four whole years for him to teach that phrase to Othello, but it was one of his favorites. Othello took off at a half jog that was *just* fast enough to have a cool wind against Mick's face but not enough that he truly had to concentrate on his rhythm. It was exactly what he needed, and a lot of the anxiety he felt about the whole Cassidy situation faded.

If only everything could be solved so easily by riding on the back of a horse. It certainly would make Mick's life a whole lot easier.

It was at least two hours later by the time he and Othello rolled right back into the barn; his spirits thoroughly lifted. He would have normally stayed out for at least three, but for some reason his back started *throbbing* about halfway through.

It was probably just his body getting used to working again.

The chores on the ranch were demanding, even if they were what he liked to do.

Othello was particularly affectionate as Mick took his gear off, sniffing at his hair and nipping at his shirt.

"Hey, calm down there, buddy. I love you too." But the horse nickered, mouthing at Mick's hair again. "I hope that means you love me too."

Mick felt a strange sort of exhaustion curl into his stomach. Fatigue was starting to hit him like a truck; he must have really tuckered himself off with all that brush clearing. He'd have to clear the water stoppage tomorrow. He'd forgotten all about asking Cassidy how she wanted it handled.

"Look, behave yourself while I brush you, okay? I kinda wanna shower and hit the hay."

Othello's head perked up at 'hay,' and Mick couldn't help but chuckle. Trust a horse to answer to that.

Thankfully, however, he did indeed keep his mouth to himself while Mick took care of him, only nickering softly when his owner brought him water for his trough. By the time he finished feeding Othello, his knees were starting to ache too.

"Hey, I'll have to catch you tomorrow. I'm right wiped out."

Othello gave a grave nod and Mick headed home, the walk to his camper seeming bizarrely wrong. Had he gone too long without eating? Maybe. Blood sugar drops could be taxing.

As soon as he was in the door, he made himself a peanut butter sandwich and wolfed it down. He could have been wrong, but his throat was beginning to prickle like it did whenever allergy season started. But it wasn't anywhere near allergy season on the western side of the cottonwood, at least as far as he knew.

Oh well. It wasn't anything a good shower and long night's rest couldn't fix.

12

Cassidy

Apologies, miss, but I need to take a sick day. I have a bug.

*C*ass stared at the single text Mick had sent her while she worked on her omelet, her brain whirring so hard she was surprised that steam didn't come out of her nostrils.

It had been two weeks since the whole touching thing, so she'd been giving the man space, only watching him work once and then dismissing herself when it was just too awkward. She hadn't meant to violate his personal space, and she felt pretty awful about it. She was the one who paid his checks, and she'd pawed at him like she owned him.

Gross.

She's almost expected him to quit, or try to sue them, but

nope. The only thing he did was stick to his work and that giant horse of his.

...and avoid the main house even more than he had before.

Was his sick day just him trying to find another job? His way of delaying quitting? She wished she knew. But even if he was, that was his right, and she wouldn't try to get in his way.

SORRY TO HEAR! *Feel better.*

IT WASN'T the best text back, but it was nonconfrontational. Or at least that was what she thought until suddenly he was calling her phone.

Had... had she done something wrong? *Again?*

Hesitantly, she answered the phone, expecting some sort of diatribe on the other side. Instead, Mick's voice was almost sheepish as he spoke.

"Look, I don't want to be a bother, but I was hoping it wouldn't be presumptuous to ask if someone could look after Othello for the day. Just feed him, talk to him, and fill his trough with water."

Oh. Oh *no.* If Mick was asking someone to take care of that horse he so clearly loved, then he really had to be sick.

"Yeah, yeah, of course. Don't worry! I'll have Charlie look after him."

"Thanks, I appreciate it," he answered in a dry rasp before disconnecting.

Geez. Poor guy.

Quickly, before she could forget, she sent off a text to Charlie and went about her day. She had physical therapy again anyway, so soon she'd be covered in sweat and longing for her shower.

But as her day went on, the man wouldn't leave her thoughts. She kept imagining him lying in his camper, too sick to even check on the horse he so clearly loved.

After long enough, she decided that she was going to just cook him some good ol' fashioned sick food. Nothing like a lil' comfort to ease his suffering.

Determined, Cass rolled herself to the kitchen, beginning to pull out different pots and pans. She was no Clara, but Papa had always insisted that no child of his wouldn't know how to make themselves a meal, so she knew her way around well enough.

Soup. Definitely some soup. Maybe some plain biscuits to absorb stomach acid? Sure, why not. Cass was so intent in her preparation that she didn't realize that Charlie had come in until his hands were on her shoulders.

"Hey there, what'cha up to, troublemaker?"

"Making some food for Mick."

"Oh yeah, you wanted me to look after his horse. He alright?"

"Sick, apparently. I thought I would help."

"By poisoning him?"

Cass slapped at his arm. "I am not *that* bad a cook."

"I mean, sure, no one's ever *died* from your cooking," Charlie joked with that impish sort of grin of his. He was so *snarky,* her little brother. "Alright, alright. I'll cut it out. Need me to grab you anything?"

"Yeah, actually, do you mind getting the onions from the larder and then the crockpot from the top cabinet?"

"I can do that."

Cass shot him a grin as she began her own prep, pulling

chicken breasts from the fridge and cutting up fresh vegetables. Once more, she was reminded of old times, just like she had been with Charity. There was a soothing sort of nature to it, and once again, she felt a little bit of her anger slip away.

Maybe... maybe she wasn't quite as limited as she thought. Sure, she couldn't run around, and she very much needed Mick's help, but that didn't mean she couldn't do most of the things she used to love.

"I think it's real nice of you to make this for the guy."

"Just figured it would be helpful," she murmured, trying not to think of how she was sort of apologizing for getting a bit handsy with the man.

"Oh, I'm sure it is. You know, between this and Clara, I've been inspired lately."

"Really?"

"Yeah, I mean between all her work with the charity and that one lightning guy, she's doing a lot of good. I feel like maybe I should do some charity stuff too."

"I mean, it couldn't hurt, right?"

Despite her cheerful comment, Cass couldn't help but feel a pang in her chest. She was hardly helpful with anything really. Especially not compared to Clara. It almost made her feel like an imposter when it came to her little brother being 'inspired' by her.

"I mean it could, but I don't think it'll be that bad. Let me know if you hear about anything through the grapevine."

"I'll do that. Would you turn the chicken breast for me?"

"Sure. I'll try not to throw it on the floor."

They shared a mild laugh together and sank into occasional conversation right up until the entire kitchen smelled absolutely delicious.

"Man, save some of this for me when I come back."

"Oh, are you heading out already?"

"Yeah, gotta take care of the horses, then do a checkup with Alejandro."

"Oh, he finally got you to come in?"

"I've been dodging him for a year, but yeah. Basically, he's holding a golfing trip hostage so I gotta pony up and let him do a checkup."

"I don't understand why you've suddenly developed such a fear of doctors," Cass remarked offhandedly. As siblings, they'd all gone for their yearly checkups together when they were teenagers and Charlie had never had a problem. But ever since he'd returned from his one semester at college... well, suddenly he refused to go.

And it wasn't just a casual, "I'm too busy." No, he would go pale, make up strange excuses, and occasionally even yell that he was doing just fine. Which, of course, meant that he was absolutely *not* fine.

"It's not doctors, Cass. It just... I don't like it when people get all pokey with me, alright? I don't wanna be touched without permission or because I have to be. It makes me..." He trailed off, the wind going right out of his sails. "Uncomfortable."

The sudden anger in his response was unexpected and Cass cleared her throat conspicuously. There it was again. It was so hot and sharp that she felt like there had to be something else to the story, but whatever it was, Charlie clearly felt no need to explain.

"Sorry. I'm just on edge, that's all."

"It's okay." She'd lashed out at all of her siblings plenty and they'd been more understanding than she deserved. It was her chance to repay the favor, so she took a tactic from Clara's book and easily changed the subject. "I understand. Seeing me in the hospital was probably pretty upsetting."

There it was, turn the conversation to giving him a logical reason to be upset that was outside of himself. It took the pressure off him and validated his response. Or at least that was what Cass hoped. And it did seem to work, Charlie smiling bashfully at her. Sometimes she forgot that he was only three years younger than her.

"Yeah, uh... that's what it is. Scary times."

"Scary times indeed."

He bent down, allowing her to press a kiss to his cheek. She really loved her brother, and she hoped his checkup went fine. The last thing their family needed was bad news about health.

"Catch you later!"

With that, he was out the door and Cass was left to her own devices.

It was strangely therapeutic, in a way. Slicing the chicken and grilling it, chopping the veggies and letting them reduce in the chicken stock Clara almost always had in the fridge. It didn't take long for the kitchen to smell even better, which Cass definitely enjoyed as she went about making the simple biscuits.

She didn't even know if Mick *could* eat them, because she didn't know what kind of sick he was. Flu? Cold? The plague? Well, probably not that last one, but she would just have to bring some of everything and hope she had whatever he needed. She knew what it was like to be knocked on her backside by unexpected health complications.

It wasn't exactly a speedy process, but at least she was able to leave it in the crockpot as she went to physical therapy, then showered after. By the time she was clean, dressed, and able to physically walk, it was definitely around dinner time. But also, early enough that no one but Papa was around.

Perfect.

Packaging everything up, she put the soup into one of their biggest thermoses and grabbed a few other things before heading out to her moped. It was just beginning to grow dark, but not so much that she was worried about toppling her ride over in a ditch or anything like that.

And so, with everything gathered, she headed out towards Mick's camper.

13

Mick

*M*ick felt awful.

Truly, grossly, utterly awful.

Mick knew he shouldn't have gone into the one bar in town, considering that he hadn't really interacted with the locals nearly enough to get immunity to their particular set of germs, but he'd wanted to get away. He wanted to drink by himself and maybe throw some darts while listening to other people complain about their lives and spend way too much money on cheap beer. Was that so bad?

Another wave of nausea rolled through him and yes, apparently it was so bad.

He'd woken up royally ill and, other than lie in bed and text Cassidy, he hadn't done much of anything else.

Other than suffer, that was.

Sometimes his body felt like it was burning from the inside

out, and sometimes it felt like someone had dumped ice-cold water over it. He was slowly cooking in his own skin, but there was nothing he could do about it.

Ugh.

That beer definitely had not been worth it.

But the whole thing had been because his mind had kept returning to that simple touch over and over again, replaying it in his head until it was some exaggerated thing. He knew he was completely overreacting, and yet...

So yeah. He'd gone to the bar hoping that some time away from the ranch might do him some good. Besides, what was the point in earning the big bucks if he never treated himself?

Well, he certainly regretted treating himself now. He was covered in a cold sweat and felt weaker than a newborn kitten, his stomach roiling violently.

Ugh, he was so hungry and thirsty, but the idea of trying to get anything along those lines made him practically dizzy with nausea. He was in a bad way.

Time was slippery in his misery, seeming to mush together yet also drag on impossibly, throwing him into some other reality where only fever and full body discomfort existed. Naturally, he was shocked when someone interrupted his misery with a knock on his door.

Mick groaned, because it was about all he could get out. What could anyone possibly want from him while he was dying? Wasn't there some sort of commandment about not disturbing a man while he was in his sickbed? If not, there needed to be.

"Hello! It's Cass. May I come in?"

Cassidy? Why was she there? He'd told her he was sick; did she not believe him?

He licked his chapped lips, trying to tell her to leave him alone, when she started talking again.

"I brought you a care package since you're so sick. I can just leave it on your steps if you like."

Only belatedly did he realize how silly it was that she was talking to him through his door, and he summoned the energy to call out to her. "Come in."

But then, as soon as he ground out those words, he realized that the steps up into his camper were going to be a real problem for her wheelchair.

His door opened, however, and for several long moments no one came in. Then, there was a metallic sound that he couldn't place, and one footstep, then another.

After what felt like ages, Cassidy slowly stepped in, using her walker to keep her balance. She was clearly fresh from the shower, dressed in soft athletic clothes and almost looking like some sort of patron Saint of Healing in the soft light of his single lamp.

Goodness, she was beautiful. Why was he always making himself ignore that? Seemed like a sin not to appreciate such lovely art from God's hands.

"One second. I just gotta get in." There were a few more huffs, and few more puffs and then she was fully inside of his camper. Yet, for supposedly having brought a care package, he didn't see any sort of food or bag with her. "Boy, that should not have been so hard," she panted, puffing air up into her slight bangs.

It was a cute action, sure, but he could only stare at her in care package-less befuddlement until he saw she had a cord tied around her wrist. Why... was she tied to something?

Suddenly those intense eyes were on him again. Didn't anyone ever tell her that she shouldn't look at sick people like that? He felt like his heart was gonna pound out of his weakened chest right then and there, even if her gaze was paired with a light smile.

"Hey there, Mick. Not to be rude, but you don't look so hot."

It took so much of his energy to answer, and yet he managed to slowly strangle out the words from the desert that was his mouth. "Strange, because I definitely feel hot."

She chuckled as she crossed to the one chair he had, sitting down in it. "I'm glad you are able to maintain your sense of humor."

"Yeah, delirium can do a lot for comedy."

She laughed slightly again, looking around as she caught her breath in the chair she'd practically collapsed into. Mick couldn't help but wonder if she was judging him, but when her attention finally turned back to him, it was *her* cheeks that were pink.

"Don't laugh, okay?" she murmured before pulling at the rope. "The extra weight throws me off balance."

Extra weight? Laugh? What was going on?

His sluggish mind grew even more confused until the rope brought a medium-sized bag right up to his door and then over the threshold. Carefully, Cassidy pulled it across the floor and up into her lap before she started carefully emptying its contents.

Oh... that explained the rope. Why didn't Mick think about that? It was pretty genius, or at least that was how it seemed to his fever-addled mind.

"Do you know what's going on with you?"

He didn't know and he didn't come up with an answer before she started pulling two thermoses out along with several sports drinks and what looked like... medicine?

"Okay, so I wasn't sure what you needed, if you have a cold, a stomach bug or what, so I just kind of emptied our entire downstairs medicine cabinet and hauled it over. I also wasn't sure how bad it was. Do you want me to call a hospital? I don't know if your benefits have officially been set up yet, but we'll cover whatever you need to get you healthy."

A spike of adrenaline shot through him and that was about the last thing he needed. "No! No hospitals!"

Cass paused at that, setting her things down and folding her hands carefully in her lap. "Mick," she said slowly, as if she was picking out every word very carefully. "You're a grown man so I trust you to be responsible for your own health, but will you promise me that you will tell me if you get sick enough to need to go?"

Sure, he could promise that. Because he *wasn't* going to get sick enough to go. He was just hit with a 24-hour bug with a nasty attitude; he was sure of it.

"...yeah."

"Alright then. Thank you, Mick. I appreciate that. I also made some biscuits, but I'm not sure if they're something you'll be able to swallow. Your throat sounds rough. Have you been coughing?"

He shook his head, barely having forgotten about the scratch and burn in his throat until she mentioned it. That probably *was* something bad, but he was distracted from that thought by her confession that she'd made him *biscuits*.

Despite the sludge in his head, Mick had enough where-withal to be touched by the gesture. She really didn't have to, especially considering how he'd been avoiding her for the past two weeks, and yet she had anyway. She really was a kind spirit. Was it so bad that she'd just barely touched him once?

"So, before I pester you on medication, how about I get

some homemade chicken noodle soup and electrolytes into you?"

Mick managed a nod, and thankfully, that seemed to be all she needed. Untying herself from her pack, she stood and slowly walked into his tiny kitchenette, using the counters as supports to keep herself straight.

It... made him feel a certain type of way to see her shakily but determinedly go about feeding him. Cassidy had been through something awful, lived in incredible pain, and yet *she* was attending to *him*? He probably would have felt selfish if he was alive enough to process more than one emotion at a time.

And yet he didn't move, couldn't do anything but lay there and sweat. Some cowboy he'd turned into.

14

Cassidy

$\mathcal{I}$t was a bit nerve-wracking being in Mick's home. But seeing him look so thoroughly wrung out and needy bolstered her to ignore the uncertainty trying to pull at her resolve. Sure, it still whispered to her that she was making him uncomfortable, but at least she was also making him *food*. She could make sure he ate and then get right out of his hair.

Puttering around, she grabbed a bowl, a spoon and a straw, figuring she should cover all her bases. The RV was cozy, but obviously run down, and she couldn't help but wonder if Charity would be able to fix some of the parts of it. She was real handy that way. Papa always said that if there was something that had a couple of interconnecting parts that Charity would want to separate them to figure out how to put it all back together.

Goodness, but Charity would sure be mad that Cass had

visited the guy while he was so sick. She could practically hear the lecture playing about her ears already.

Oh well, if Charity wanted to grump, she could grump after Mick was all cared for.

Grabbing everything she needed, she headed over to his bed that took up the back part of the camper. Setting the stuff down on his nightstand took about three more trips than she would have liked, and then she was carefully moving the chair over so she could sit. It was definitely one of the most strenuous things she had done in a while, and she could already feel sweat pouring down her back. At least she'd chosen to wear comfortable athletic gear.

"You really don't have to," Mick groaned and goodness, if his pained voice didn't just stab straight through her heart. Ow. He sounded absolutely miserable. Maybe she could get him a cool washcloth and—

Focus. Food first.

"I'm just looking out for my fellow man. Here, let me prop you up a little."

It took some adjusting, with his arms shaking as much as hers, but eventually she got his upper half at an angle where he could eat. Without thinking, Cass dumped some of the soup into the bowl, dunked the spoon in, then offered the nearly overflowing utensil to him.

Oh... she was trying to feed a grown man like a baby, wasn't she?

Mick sent her a weary look, but somehow Cass managed to level him with a blank stare. He hesitated for maybe a moment more, but his mouth was closing around the spoon.

She watched the dark column of his throat as it bobbed, then hurriedly got him another spoonful. He didn't hesitate on the second offering, and quickly swallowed that down.

"Wow, you have no idea how good that feels."

Relief flooded her at that, and maybe even a hint of pride. "Mama used to feed us this when we were real young and sick. Always made me feel better."

He nodded, then eagerly took another mouthful. Then another. It was after about six or so that she set the bowl to the side.

"Let's go nice and easy, okay? What about sipping one of these next?" She offered him the sports drink and a straw, already having removed the top.

"You've just thought of everything, haven't you?"

Already his voice was sounding stronger and talking seemed to be coming more easily to him. Thank goodness. Cass hated to think of just how awful he would have felt if she hadn't visited. He definitely was dehydrated and that always made everything worse.

"Well, I figured if I was going to haul my crippled self out here, I better make sure I didn't leave anything behind."

"Fair point," he said, shooting her a weary smile that made her blood seem to race faster than it should. It was just because she'd exerted herself so much, of course. That was the only reason her heart had decided to start beating so fast she could practically hear it.

Fortunately, it was quite easy to distract herself from that rush by watching him slowly sip through the straw, his eyes closing in relief. Color started to flood his ashen cheeks, returning that beautiful dark hue to him instead of making him look gray and withered.

"Wow, look how much you've perked up already. I bet if we can get this whole bowl into you, that you'll be right as rain."

"Well, I don't think I'll be doing cartwheels anytime soon, but I do feel better."

"I'm real glad to hear that, Mick. Think you're ready for some more soup?"

He nodded slowly, those dark eyes of his regarding her with something she couldn't quite name, but she didn't waver. She gripped the bowl again and rested it on the edge of the bed, her other hand guiding the spoon to Mick's mouth.

She didn't hurry, making sure he went at an even pace that wouldn't upset his stomach, but he only made it through half the bowl before shaking his head.

"It's delicious, but I think I just need to rest now. Ain't never been so sick that just eating tuckered me out."

"That's okay, you did really good."

Cass knew that she should set the bowl and utensils within his reach then leave, but she didn't want to. Somehow, it just didn't seem like *enough*.

"Would you like a cool washcloth? Something to take the heat off your face?"

The look he sent her was one of pure gratitude. "I wouldn't say no to that."

"Alright, you wait right there."

"Honestly, don't think I'd be going anywhere else even if I wanted to."

She chuckled at that. When Mick opened up, he sure was funny. It was just too bad that those moments were so few and far between.

"If at any point you want me to head out, just let me know. Wouldn't wanna overstay my welcome."

"You just being here. I imagine that wasn't easy."

But Cass just shrugged. "Your place is your place. Besides, rest is gonna be pretty crucial for you for the next few days, I imagine. Well, that and hydration."

"Yes, ma'am."

Her eyes flicked to him to make sure he wasn't being sarcastic, but he wasn't. There was only a soft sort of expression across his handsome features.

Oh goodness, why did that make her heart skip a beat? She didn't know, and she rushed to get that cool washcloth so she could distract herself for a few moments.

First things first, finding an actual washcloth would help.

There were only two other doors in the place, and one of them was clearly one of those slatted wooden ones that almost always was in front of pantries, so she guessed the second one had to lead to the bathroom.

Ugh, going into a bachelor's bathroom. Cass had never really been in one before, considering she'd always lived at home, but she'd heard some real stories. Did she need galoshes? A hazmat suit?

Carefully, she opened the door and heaved a sigh of relief. It was incredibly tiny, with only a cramped shower booth, a short toilet and the skinniest sink she'd ever seen.

"You look like you were expecting a monster or something," Mick murmured from the bed.

"Sorry. I've watched too many intervention shows where the bathrooms could fuel nightmares."

"So you finally have a flaw."

Cass blinked at him, half into the doorway. "What?"

"You watch trashy tv."

"Mick, I don't know what kind of impression I've made on you, but I certainly have many, *many* more flaws than my choice in late-night television."

"Come now, miss, don't lie."

Her eyes went wide. What was she lying about!?

"We both know you can't stay up past ten."

That wasn't what she was expecting at all and the startled

laugh burst out of her mouth. "You really had me going there for a moment, you know that?"

"Really? Why? You got secrets you're hiding?"

Cassidy laughed aloud again.

Ducking into his bathroom, she grabbed a cloth then took it to the kitchen, wetting it down then sticking it in the freezer.

"Would you like some tea? I brought it in the other thermos."

"I think I'm good with this drink, but I don't mind you having a cup with me."

"I don't mind that at all."

Grabbing a mug from his counter and rinsing it, she grabbed the cool cloth from the freezer, then stumbled her way over to him. Carefully, she laid it over his forehead, not missing how goosebumps rose along his arms.

"How's that?"

"Refreshing."

"Good. You drink your drink now."

He raised an eyebrow but did as she asked, slowly sipping at it as she poured her own tea. Sure, the chair she was settled in wasn't really that comfortable, but she settled back anyway, quietly sipping her sweet tea.

"You know all that sugar isn't good for you," Mick remarked, that low rumble just barely returning to his voice. But goodness, it still affected her just as much.

"You hush now. You're sick."

"That doesn't mean—"

"Drinky drinky."

At that *both* of his eyebrows shot up, and she dissolved into a couple snorting giggles.

"You're lucky you're charming," was all he said before sipping through his straw again.

He... he thought she was charming? That was certainly news, because she felt like she was always acting strange, unmannered or controlling with him.

She didn't argue with him and just continued to drink from her mug, watching him slowly work through his sports drink. He was still sweating, and his hand shook when he passed her the empty bottle, but at least he had some color and his words back.

"I... I think I'm about to pass out," he murmured, eyelids fluttering in a way that reminded her of how she'd been at their lunch together on her first day.

"Okay, let me just clear up and I'll get out of your hair. I'm going to leave the soup thermos by your bed. It'll be better heated up, but cold soup is better than nothing if you don't have it in you to make it to the microwave later."

"...thanks. Really."

"It's nothing, honest. If you really wanna thank me, just try to get better as best you can."

He nodded and that was enough for her. Muscles still sore, she finished picking things up, then bundled it up to go back out the door and on her moped.

"Speedy recovery, Mick," Cass said softly, the man's eyes already closed. With one last moment of lingering, she finally saw herself out and closed the door behind her.

15

Cassidy

*M*ick did not get better.

Three days passed with Cassidy visiting him each night, and he was still as sick as a dog. Sure, he would perk up while she fed him, got electrolytes in him and plied him with even more cool washcloths. But when she inevitably came back, he was always just as bad as the previous time.

They talked, as much as it seemed difficult for him to do so, and once Charlie even brought Othello up to the window. The horse had made concerned noises, but Cass didn't miss how Mick lit up. He loved that horse; that much was obvious. Maybe one day she'd get to hear the story of them.

But first, he had to beat whatever was ailing him.

Cass vaguely remembered reading in the hospital that men were more susceptible to extreme symptoms of certain illnesses like colds and flu, which was why they seemed to suffer so intensely. She read up on more things to bolster his immune system and headed out for a fourth night of care, hoping that maybe, just maybe, he'd finally turned the corner.

But as she arrived and wobbled up his steps, she nearly fell right back out of it when she saw he wasn't in his bed.

"Mick!?" she called in alarm, all sorts of impossible theories from kidnapping to alien abduction suddenly popping into her head. But a noise sounded from the bathroom, and she rushed to the tiny room, knocking over her walker in the process. "Mick! Oh. There you are."

He managed a groan, and Cass wasn't quite sure how she got on the floor, but suddenly she was on her knees beside him.

He seemed lethargic and his eyes were closed as he curled up on the cool vinyl floor. Mick, can you open your eyes and look at me?"

Again, no answer. Right. Desperate times then. She could call her sister and drive him to the hospital, but the closest one was about an hour and a half away. There was an urgent care in the next town over, but why waste all that time when she had someone much closer?

Hurriedly yanking out her phone, she hit Alejando's contact and begged for him to pick up. One ring. Two rings. Finally, on the third he answered, sounding sleepy.

Strange, it was just past seven. Maybe he had been napping after a long day in the office? She remembered Charity saying that he didn't sleep nearly enough.

"Cass? Are you okay?"

"It's not me. It's our ranch hand. Something's wrong with him."

She was grateful that Alejandro knew her well enough not

to question why she'd chosen to call him instead of an ambulance. "What's going on? Was there an accident?"

"No, nothing like that. He's been sick for days and I think it's getting worse than better. He doesn't seem to be able to talk right now, and he's curled up on the floor of his RV."

"Temperature?"

Cass reached around him and felt for his forehead. He was dripping in sweat but clammy. Like a dead fish. She told Alejandro as much and his tongue clicked.

"Right, I'll be there right away. Try to put a cool cloth on the back of his neck. Thanks for calling me, Cass."

"Of course. You're family. I know I can count on you."

She could almost hear his pleased flush on the other end of the line. "I appreciate that. I'm heading out the door now."

Good. That was good. Hanging up, Cass rushed to get another washcloth. By the time she had it on Mick's neck, his eyes fluttered open once to look at her, then closed again.

"Hey, help is on the way. It'd make me feel a whole lot better if you could just tell me how you are, though."

"*Drink*," he finally managed in a ragged gasp.

Drink! That Cass could do. She grabbed at the rope tied around her wrist and yanked it up into the trailer, then dragged it to the bathroom. Hands shaking, she practically ripped it open and snatched a bottle out.

But when she went to open it, all the adrenaline and stress clearly decided that it was their time to strike. As much as she tried to curl her fingers around the top, they wouldn't cooperate. Between the trembling and the cramping, her hand refused to do what she wanted it to do.

"Fine then," she spat with vehemence. She wasn't going to let her body stop her from helping!

Teeth it was then. It certainly didn't feel great and her

mouth hurt, but after a few moment's work, she finally managed to unscrew it enough to pop the lid off. Man, her dentist was *not* going to be happy with her.

"Here, here, I got you. Can you lean back a bit? I'll hold it."

Mick must have heard her, but he didn't seem to get the 'a bit' part, practically collapsing backward into the wall of the shower stall.

"Whoa there! Here, let me help!"

She managed to slide one shaking leg behind his back and curl an arm woodenly around his shoulder while her other hand brought the drink up to his mouth. If he noticed how badly she was trembling, her fingers bent oddly around the bottle, he didn't say. No, he just tilted his head back and let her pour a few drops into his mouth.

It seemed to take forever and *so* much energy for him to swallow. It made her heart hurt, a throbbing, worried feeling, to see him struggle to complete a basic biological task. Mick didn't deserve all that.

"Don't worry, I've got you. You're doing great," she soothed, waiting a few more beats before tilting the bottle again. "We can take this as slow as you need. Don't worry."

And they did take it slow. Time lost its meaning, the passage of it only measured by sips and swallows. Cass watched him so hard she was sure she would strain her eyes, but that didn't matter. No, the only thing that was important was Mick drinking just a little more.

She wished there was something more she could do. She wished she could magically heal him or at least know *how* he was actually sick. She wished *so* many things, but as usual, she was practically useless.

That was something she was used to since her accident.

16

Mick

$\mathcal{L}$ife was blurry and strange for entirely too long, a discordant string of noises, sounds and unpleasant sensations. His skin burned, but it was also freezing, making him more nauseous than he had ever been in his life.

Part of him was aware that Cassidy was there, and it was her cool hand that often gripped his. Her voice was distorted, but occasionally her words made it through the haze. She kept telling him he would be alright.

And despite the pain, despite the burning, he believed her.

The delirium was intense, however, robbing him of speech and most consciousness. He slipped between memories, things that had never happened to him and awful nightmares with only brief trips to reality. It almost made him wonder if he'd died and was stuck in some sort of awful limbo, and somewhere in the gaps, that made him think.

He had so much that he wanted to *do*.

He'd been wandering, lost, for so long. Without purpose, trying to find a place that made the listlessness in his soul settle. He was nearly thirty years old and he hadn't accomplished anything besides buying Othello, the horse's trailer, and his RV. If he really was dead, he didn't have a legacy. Didn't have anything for anyone to remember him by.

...and that was a real shame.

Eventually, those little flashes of reality grew longer. Wider. And his sleep was more peaceful and less a kaleidoscopic hellscape of sensation. Although he didn't know how many days had passed when his eyes eventually cracked open, he wasn't surprised to see it was daytime. Last he remembered, the sun had just set, so it made sense that it had to be at least the next day.

He realized his throat was so raw that it was impossible to form a single word.

Well, that would just have to wait until later, so he closed his eyes and slept again.

The next time they opened, he was more lucid. Lucid enough to realize that he felt like he had been hit by a truck. He tried to turn his head, but the command didn't quite make it, so he sank back into slumber again.

A third time. A fourth time. It wasn't until the fifth time where he actually felt fully human and movement in the corner of his vision caught his attention.

He was still in his RV. Part of him thought that he would come to in some sort of shining, sterilized hospital. Glancing to the side, he realized that there *was* an IV hooked up to him that was hanging from the ceiling. So... there was a doctor around then?

There was that movement again and he squinted against

the daylight to look deeper into his camper, wondering if it was the same day he'd first woken up or another one entirely.

Mick tried to lick his lips to speak, only to realize that they were practically sandpaper and his tongue stuck to them for a moment. Thankfully, someone seemed to notice that he was awake because a man was walking towards him.

"Hey there, you have some good timing. I just got here to check up on you."

Check up on him? So was Mick looking at the doctor he'd heard so much about?

"I'm fairly certain that the simple fact that you're alive means that you have viral meningitis instead of bacterial, but I would much prefer if we could go to the hospital and test this out."

Hospital? No. Hospitals were where people went to die. His own nana had gone in for something that should have been simple, but doctors were so busy ignoring her and telling her that she needed to lose weight, that they misidentified her symptoms and made her time in their care utter misery.

Mick closed his eyes against the memories. He remembered fighting with doctors for her to be released, then trying to find someone, anyone who would treat her *and* listen to her. He didn't know if it was because she was poor or black. Or both.

So no. Never, *ever*.

"No hospitals," he gasped, his throat feeling like paper.

"Are you certain? In order to test it, you need a lumbar puncture, and that's not really something we should do here. At all."

"No. Hospitals."

"I respect your words; I just want to make sure you understand. You could just have viral meningitis which is something your body works through. You could have bacterial. However, it's less likely you have that one, because it's lethal within a few days, and you're on day seven, according to Cass."

Day seven!? That meant that he'd been dipping in and out of consciousness for three days. That was both terrifying and somewhat impossible to believe. He'd lost a week to being sick?

"However, your symptoms are *quite* severe, and that makes me nervous."

"It's probably the diabetes," Mick managed to gasp, and the doctor's eyebrows practically shot off his head.

"Pardon me, but did you say you have diabetes?"

"Type one. Had it since a kid. Ties into the whole heart thing."

Suddenly the doctor was looking sharply to the kitchen. "You didn't tell me that he had diabetes. That's quite an important thing I would have liked to be informed of."

"I didn't know!" Cassidy's voice answered, sounding panicked. "You have diabetes?"

Blinking, Mick squinted some more and saw her leaning heavily on her walker while standing at his stove, stirring something. He was pretty sure that it probably smelled heavenly, but his nose was somehow both dryer than a bone and incredibly congested.

"It's not exactly something I advertise. I just figured you saw my glucose meter on my belt and didn't pry."

"Your what? The weird pager thing you wear?"

"That's... that's not a pager. Who has a pager nowadays?"

"I dunno. Strange cowboys from the east coast."

If it were any other time, he might have laughed. But

considering he still felt like an overstretched, overcooked and overtwisted noodle, he only managed a weak smile. "Well, no. It's not a pager. It helps me keep track of my blood sugar and the like."

"Well, you are correct," the doctor cut in. "Diabetes would indeed make your symptoms worse. Now, I'm willing not to call an ambulance and rush you out of here, whether you like it or not, if you make me one promise."

Mick affixed the doctor with the firmest glare he could, but he had the feeling most of the power just wasn't there. "And what's that?"

"If you get any sicker than you feel right now, you go to a hospital of your own free will. But, as long as you continue to slowly improve, I'll keep seeing you here."

They exchanged a long, long stare before Mick finally nodded once. "I think that's reasonable."

"Good. Now, I've got an IV on you because you were severely dehydrated. Do you think you're up for drinking everything you need to on your own, or do you want it to stay on for just one more day?"

Mick swallowed, which turned out to hurt more than swallowing ever should, which made him wince, and it turned out wincing hurt too. Being sick *wasn't cool*. "Let's leave it another day."

"Alright then. You've done an amazing job so far, so just keep resting as much as you can. I'll see myself out."

At that the doctor returned to the kitchen, saying several things to Cass too low for Mick to make out. He was sure that, if he strained, he could probably decipher the words. But the idea of straining for *anything* made him want to recoil inside of himself, so he just laid there.

A few minutes later, the doctor headed out, leaving just him and Cassidy.

"Hey there," she murmured, shuffling over to him with her walker. Her face was drawn and there were dark circles under her eyes, but she still smiled at him like seeing him was the best thing in the world. "Can I get you some ice chips to suck on? Your mouth must be pretty dry."

He nodded, watching as she slowly made her way back into his kitchen and the slender freezer that he had. He wanted to tell her he didn't have any ice chips at all, but then she was pulling out a bowl that was filled with exactly that. Huh, she'd been busy since he was out, hadn't she?

"Have you been here the whole time?" he managed to croak out, the question coming out perhaps a tad more bluntly than it should have. But the thought that she'd taken care of him, stayed by his side, even called a doctor to help him had something strange simmering in his chest.

"Well, I mean, I went home for ingredients and showers and the like. And Charlie did a couple night shifts so I could nap back home. Your folding chair isn't exactly the comfiest."

Wow. That... that was mind-boggling. She'd been with him for nearly four days, with him sweating in a delirious fog. How... that was insane. Generous, but insane. Nobody just did that for a stranger.

"Aren't you putting yourself at risk?" He was pretty sure that she had mentioned something about her immune system being weak from the trauma and still recovering, but he couldn't be sure.

Naturally, he was pretty surprised when she laughed, but the smile on her face was genuine. "One school year all five of us Miller children got meningitis at once. It was, horrible." She shook her head, chuckling again as she recounted the memories. "It's pretty rare to ever get it twice, so everything should be good."

"Oh..."

"I was just cooking up some simple broth in the hopes you might wake up today. Think you're up for some if I give you a bottle and a straw?"

Mick couldn't help but stare at her, so many things churning through him that it felt like it was about to over-whelm his still-recovering brain. Maybe, if he wasn't so fried and frazzled, it would make more sense. But as it were, he could only stare at her in wonder.

And it was probably because of his poor, recovering brain that he was blurting out again.

"Why?"

"I mean, you heard Alejandro. You need to stay hydrated, and I figured broth was a good way to get some calories *and* some fluids in you."

"No, I meant..." He took a deep breath, trying to order his thoughts. "I mean why did you stay here? You could have..." She could have done lots of things, actually. She never had to visit in the first place, and she could have stopped at any time. She could have just called an ambulance to be rid of him. She could have... but she didn't.

Slowly, she made her way to his side and sat down. "You were in need and I could help. I know I may not be able to do much, but if I can help someone, I'm going to. Especially if they're someone I'm responsible for."

Ah, so it was just responsibility, not because he was impor-tant to her. But even though a bitter part of him thought that, most of him was still filled with a warm sort of fuzziness.

...or maybe that was the meningitis.

"Look, you get some rest and I'll bottle up some of the

broth for later. I'll be here when you wake up, I promise. Until you're ready for me to go, you're stuck with me."

Mick smiled, and maybe if he were himself, he would have said something flattering back. But as it were, he just closed his eyes and slipped back into his dreams.

Hopefully, they would be nicer to him.

17

Cassidy

*D*iabetes! Mick had *diabetes*, and apparently that made meningitis go into overdrive.

Goodness gracious, she couldn't believe it. She'd almost killed him! She should have sent him packing to a hospital despite his protests. They could have hooked him up to an especially good IV right away and he wouldn't have gotten so dehydrated or lost so much weight.

Because he had *definitely* lost a shocking amount of weight. His face was gaunt and his normally royal bone structure had taken on a more severe look. And goodness, what about his *blood sugar!?* Cass didn't know much about diabetes, either type 1 or 2, but she did know that maintaining blood sugar was important to the disease.

What if she'd made him sick? What if she made him go into... what was the word? Hypoglycemic? That seemed right.

Cass couldn't help but feel like she'd royally bungled the whole thing, and the guilt certainly was eating at her.

"Have you been up this whole time?"

Cass looked up from where she was curled on the couch, a throw blanket over her and her messy nest of pillows.

"Oh, hey, Charlie." Cass stretched, yawning slightly. "What time is it?"

"It's three in the morning. I haven't seen you up this late since—"

Cass knew exactly what he had been going to say. "Since my accident?"

"Yeah, since your accident."

"You're not wrong. But no wonder I'm so exhausted. Help me up, will you?"

"Sure!" Charlie hustled over to her, getting her onto her feet and over to her walker. Her shoulders were incredibly sore and stiff, but other than that she was mostly recovered from the previous week's PT. "What was keeping you up anyway."

"I was reading about diabetes."

"That's an interesting topic. Any reason?"

Cass stopped herself from answering right away. She didn't think she had a right to spread Mick's medical info everywhere, especially since he said that he wasn't keen on advertising it.

"Information wormhole and all that, you know."

"Ah, yeah. I've fallen down the rabbit hole before and suddenly ended up on the fall of the Byzantine empire at five in the morning. It really is insane the sheer amount of information we have at our fingertips."

"Isn't it?" Cass asked, satisfied that she had successfully shifted the conversation away from Mick entirely. "I remember how in sixth grade I was taught about the Dewey Decimal system in the library and how to use reference books, then in eighth grade we spent a whole week learning how to cite articles and sources from the internet."

"You know I love it when you tell me stories about the ancient times."

She wasn't so much of an invalid that she couldn't elbow him in the side. "You're only three years younger than me."

"Yeah, but you see, the difference is that you are thirty and I'm only twenty-seven, which means that you're in your third decade of life while I am only in my second. We live in two different eras, really."

"Remind me to scare you in your sleep."

"Good luck getting over all the Legos I've scattered across the floor of my room."

"Really? Your go-to defense is a child's building block?" Although she was needling him, Cass was having fun. Charlie was always great to banter with, parked somewhere between endlessly silly and delightfully witty, his answers always managed to keep pretty much everyone on their toes.

"I mean, think about navigating your chair or walker around them and then get back to me on whether you think it's a bad idea or not."

Actually... he had a point there. Not that she would ever admit it.

"Right, well, before you turn your room into a Home Alone setup, are you willing to walk me to mine?"

"I don't see why I wouldn't be. Let me just grab a drink. It's why I came down here anyway."

"What, you forgot to fill up the mini-fridge in your room again?"

"Don't judge me. I am a busy man."

"Right, all that video gaming and rodeoing keep you real occupied."

"You bet'cha." He winked cheekily, because Charlie was always cheeky, then jogged to the kitchen.

Cass missed jogging. Sometimes it seemed like she was going to be perpetually stuck in turtle mode, but she hoped that one day she'd be back to moving at a pace that was at least a bit faster than paint drying on a wall.

Charlie, oblivious to her longing, jogged right back to her side. "Shall we?" he said, offering his arm with a corny little bow.

"Let's," she answered.

They didn't go far, as she had to stop and grab her walker by the stairs and then she didn't have a free arm for him to hold, but it was still nice, and when they ended up in her room she practically collapsed on the bed.

"Hey, Cass?"

"Yeah?"

"You know you're amazing, right?"

Although it took quite a lot of energy, Cass rolled onto her side to give him a curious look. "Please tell me that you're not going to say that seeing me walking around is inspirational."

He snorted and that certainly wasn't a sound she expected. "No, nothing like that. I just mean everything you're doing with this Mick guy. A lot of people wouldn't have gotten involved, but you basically saved his life."

"I did not," Cass objected immediately.

"What else would you call it, sis? You fed him, kept him hydrated—or at least tried—and you called a doctor when he clearly wouldn't. I don't know about you, but that's saving someone in my book."

Cass flushed, the idea sitting strangely with her. "I... I didn't do anything like that."

"What would you call it then?"

"I, uh, I was just... I dunno, helping."

"Alright, well I admire how much you helped him and I'm sure he does too. Most people wouldn't be so selfless."

Except she wasn't really selfless about it, was she? Cass couldn't deny that she was drawn to Mick, and she probably wouldn't have ended up at his camper if she wasn't, so it felt wrong to accept any kudos for it.

Basically, she'd swung into heroism as a byproduct of her little crush and touching Mick when she shouldn't have, so she didn't want praise for it.

She just wanted Mick to be healthy.

"I'd hold off on all the accolades. I was just doing what was right."

"Alright, I'm not gonna argue about semantics, but I just wanted you to know even though I'm only three years younger than you as you love to point out, I still look up to you."

Despite her disagreeing with his premise, she still flushed with affection at his words. She really was lucky to have such an amazing family. A lot of people couldn't say the same, like her cousins in Texas—although apparently that whole side of the family was going through some serious changes.

"Thanks, Charlie. I suppose you're entirely tolerable."

"Oh, be still my heart. I don't know how to handle such lavish praise."

"Sorry, I tried to play it cool there. Didn't realize the bar was so low."

He chuckled at that, shaking his head. "Good night, Cass. Get some rest, okay? I'm sure you'll be right back at Mick's tomorrow, so you'll need it."

He was right. She absolutely would be there with food and drinks and a whole lot of cool washcloths. "Night, Charlie. Good luck on beating whatever boss you're fighting against."

"It's not that kind of game, but thanks. Love you lots."

"Love you, too."

He closed her door, and she heard him walk to the stairs to head up to his attic room. Alone with her thoughts again, she said a quick prayer for Mick's health, her normal anger towards God forgetting to load until well after she said 'amen.'

18

Mick

After another long week, Mick was almost back to normal. Sure, he had some lingering weakness and stiffness from being bedridden, and he'd lost a lot of his muscle tone, but he felt he was finally ready to get back to work.

Cassidy expressed concern, of course, but it wasn't like he was jumping the gun. He had indeed woken up on that seventh day and drank her broth, and the next day the doctor had returned to remove his IV. On the ninth day he was up and shuffling to the bathroom then back, and by the tenth day he was sitting up to eat and wandering around his house.

It took him an embarrassing while to figure out that something was missing, and he squeezed his eyes shut against the idea. Unfortunately, that didn't really work, and his mind was

100% aware that the reason everything felt off was because Cassidy wasn't around.

Even though he'd been unconscious for a good part of it, he had spent nearly two weeks of dinner with her. And for the chunk he had been lucid for, she'd always been there as he'd fallen asleep for the night. For the first time since he'd bought his RV, it felt strangely empty, and that feeling followed him into slumber.

~

"HEY THERE, big guy. Did you miss me?"

Othello's head stuck out of his stall, the horse giving a mighty whinny and reared up on his hind legs so that his head cleared the top of what was essentially his bedroom. Mick grinned, sauntering over to his friend.

"I missed you too, friend."

He wasn't kidding either. If there was one thing he thought about besides being in pain or Cassidy, it was Othello. The longest he'd gone without seeing his friend was about two days, and they were just past a week. Had the draft horse thought he was abandoned, like he was before? Probably not, considering Charlie visited him multiple times a day and reported that he was well behaved the whole time, but still...

Mick unlatched the door and walked in, walking straight up to Othello and throwing his arms around the mount's neck. He couldn't quite reach around, but he could grip the horse's thick mane and press his head against the swell of Othello's warm cheek.

"It's been rough, buddy. Real rough. But I thought about you the whole time, I promise."

Othello let out a soft sound, shifting from foot to foot,

before stilling. That was another great thing about Othello; he was a tactile sort of horse. As much as he loved being told that he was handsome, strong and amazing, he also loved being patted, stroked or hugged. Really, all attention was good attention to Othello.

Mick couldn't say how long he held him, leaning into Othello's muscled form, but eventually he pulled back.

"I don't think I have a ride in me, but you want to go for a short walk? I brought a book for that one tree you like to flirt with Matilda around." Othello made an interested wuffle. "Don't give me that. I see how you've been looking at her. She's a cute little filly, so I can't say I blame you, but she's off-limits unless I actually sell your stallion services. You feel me?"

Othello gave him a dubious look, which had Mick chuckling.

"Alright, maybe a *little* flirting. But let's keep it at that on opposite sides of the fences."

The horse shook his head, flicking Mick in the face, before his head started rooting for the satchel Mick had brought.

"You know, I'm beginning to think that you just like me for my treats."

Othello neither confirmed nor denied that accusation, instead staring with impatience at Mick's bag. Laughing outright, Mick pulled an apple from the pack and held it out to his mount. Othello whinnied happily then dug in, crunching away and making a general mess of things. Once he was done, Mick wiped his hand, then pushed the stall door open.

The two of them walked out together, Othello going slower than usual when confronted with some free roam. It wasn't until they were nearly all the way out the door that Mick realized that Othello was acting like he knew his human was sick.

Actually, when the cowboy thought about it, Othello had acted strangely that night before things got bad.

Wait a minute...

"Did you know I was sick?" Mick asked in shock, looking over at his very tall companion.

But Othello just blinked at him, still plodding forward calmly. With a shrug, Mick followed after him, but he couldn't help but wonder whether his big guy had been trying to warn him.

Huh, wouldn't that be something?

They reached the spot that Mick had been aiming for, and he sat down right at the base of the tree, leaning back against the sturdy wood. Opening his book, he gave a nod to Othello— who seemed to be waiting for something—then let himself sink into the pages for a minute.

"How was your first day of work? Sorry I missed it, but you know how it is with PT and all that."

Mick was thoroughly engrossed in reading about what different parts of the brain did after a lobotomy or traumatic head injury, so he jolted, looking up to see Cassidy sitting in that special moped her sister made for her.

Oh.

He hadn't expected her to be there.

While he'd been shocked and touched by Cassidy helping him when he was sick, that feeling increased tenfold once he was healthy enough to be fully lucid. She'd spent hours and *hours* by his side, feeding him, hydrating him, talking to him, putting cool washcloths on him. It made his head spin how she'd basically become his nurse without a single complaint.

And the strange cherry on the top of everything she'd done for him was the fact that her wheelchair couldn't fit into his camper at all, so she either used her walker or his small kitchen's counters to stand and move about. While he knew that she was fairly adept with her mobility aid, he also knew how quickly she became fatigued, and that when she was fatigued, her hands would curl up and most of her extremities would start shaking and cramping.

But even with all that, she was there every day.

Incredible.

Mick wasn't used to owing people, and he was even less used to being showered in kindness, and that unfamiliarity left him not knowing what to do with Cassidy.

Not that he needed to do anything with Cassidy, but—

"Cat got your tongue?"

Oh right, he was supposed to answer. That was how conversations and normal social interaction worked. Right. He knew that. He was just... rusty. He was sure she understood; his brain was still recovering from being nearly fried, after all.

"Sorry. Was just thinking." A smooth, brilliant reply. He was an aficionado of conversation. "What are you doing out here?"

Usually Cassidy was out of order for at least a few hours after her physical therapy, especially lately. She told Mick that was a good thing, because it meant the doctor thought she was healthy enough to push, but the cowboy had his doubts. Mostly because he hated seeing how in pain and utterly drained she was after the wringing that Alejandro guy put her through.

"I actually have some beef stew in my bag that Clara made. I was wondering if maybe you needed something fortifying after a long first day back."

In all honestly, Mick had forgotten about eating entirely, although he was fairly certain he'd had both lunch and his afternoon snack. That probably wasn't the best for his health, but hey, he figured his stomach was still coming back online after five days on IV nourishment.

"You didn't have to do that," he murmured, feeling that rushing warmth spread through him. He didn't have a name for it, but goodness, it was a nice feeling.

"I don't have to do a lot of things. But I guess I'm in the habit of coming around."

Mick dogeared the page he was on then stood, brushing off his pants. "I think it's too soon to put Othello back in his stall, but I'll take him to the pen and then I'll be ready to go."

"Alright. I'll just head to your place and get things started up."

"Sounds like a plan."

It wasn't until he was halfway to walking Othello to one of the large pens for the horses that he thought about the strange familiarity his employer had with his place of residence. Mick wasn't exactly the most social person, so the last time he'd had a visitor in his camper had been at least four years earlier. But Cassidy was comfortable enough to go there without him and heat up the stew, which made sense considering that she'd visited literally every day for two weeks. That was something that would normally be reserved for a significant other.

Oh.

That was certainly a thought.

Mick shook his head. He did *not* have the time or energy to entertain ludicrous thoughts like that. So instead, he concentrated on getting Othello into the pen and handing him another apple.

One very messy hand later, Mick was heading back home.

...why did that make him nervous?

19

Mick

*A*s soon as he walked into the door, a delicious, hearty smell struck him. He imagined if he was a cartoon character that he'd be floating on the scent, but alas, such things weren't actually possible in reality.

"That smells delicious," Mick remarked, crossing to sit at the folding chair that had shown up next to his small table sometime during his illness. He guessed that either Cassidy or Alejandro had brought it, considering he'd only ever had the one other chair, but it didn't quite seem important enough to ask.

"I'll send your compliments to Clara. I'm sure she'd love to hear it."

"I imagine. She certainly seems enthusiastic about cooking."

"That's putting it mildly. I never thought I'd meet someone

who liked cooking more than Papa, but Clara might just have him."

Huh. Gardening, cooking... Mick was fully aware that hobbies didn't really have a gender—especially when it came to *food*—but he couldn't help but wonder if Papa Miller liked those things because it reminded him of the wife he lost.

Not really his business though, so he kept his mouth shut.

Or at least he did until Cassidy started talking again.

"So, I know your stomach is still sensitive, but I brought some ginger ale to switch things up. I realize that all water and sports drinks for two weeks probably has you burnt out on both of them."

She'd brought him ginger ale? His heart thumped once again at the revelation. Just how thoughtful was she? Mick was struggling with ideas on how to pay her back even slightly while she just seemed to effortlessly make his life better without even missing a beat.

"I really appreciate that. Ginger ale sounds amazing."

"Really? I'm so glad! I remember my mother used to have us drink that and eat some crackers when our stomachs were unsettled. Not sure if it's actual medicine, but it reminds me of getting better and being tended to so..." She blushed, pausing in her stirring of the stew. "Sorry, I'm babbling. You don't want to hear all this."

"No, I do," Mick answered quickly. He wasn't a talkative person by nature, but his bout with sickness had left him even less verbose than usual. But that didn't mean he didn't *want* to have a conversation with Cassidy. He was just... rusty. "I like hearing about your life."

She smiled softly at that, seeming pleased. Mick wasn't sure why what he wanted mattered to her, but he wasn't about to pester her with questions about that.

"Good to know."

"Is it?"

"Hmm?" she responded, reaching up to pull two of the three bowls he owned down from his tiny cupboard. For a moment he felt embarrassment flash through him and wondered what she thought about his scant collection.

But then he told his mind to get a hold of itself. Cassidy was the last person to care about something as banal as dishware. She had way more important things to worry about.

"Is it good to know?"

The corners of her eyes crinkled as her grin grew. "Yeah, it is."

Mick hadn't expected her to admit it was. He'd been half-expecting for her to volley a comeback at him that got him bantering. But the matter-of-fact way she said it gave him pause, and before he knew it, she was setting a steaming bowl of thick, delicious-smelling stew in front of him.

"So, I know that first night you were sicker than anything, but you perked right back up when you heard I brought biscuits."

Mick nodded. "It was a real shame those went to waste."

"Oh, don't worry, the chickens loved them once they got stale. But anyway, I bring them up because I made you a mini batch for tonight. Figure they'd go great with the stew."

Mick's mouth did indeed start to water, and boom, third strike, he felt the hardened shell around his heart crack right in two, the feelings that he'd been suppressing overwhelming his denial in an outright flood.

She'd brought him food. She'd brought him Ginger Ale. She'd nursed him to health and then, on top of everything, made *fresh* homemade biscuits for him with a honey glaze. He'd had them a couple of times before thanks to Clara's cooking, and the fact that she remembered how he'd liked them felt so incredibly significant.

And so, it was while he was staring at her over his bowl of stew that he realized he might just be in love.

Not full-blown declarations of eternity love, but a small flicker of light that he'd never felt before. But when he looked at Cassidy, he saw so many possibilities he never could have imagined before.

Too bad she's your boss, another, more cynical part of his mind supplied.

...that was true.

"I'm actually starving, so sorry if I splash you while I down this," Cassidy said, chuckling softly as she plopped into the chair across from him. Her spoon was already in her hand, and he noticed it was one of his, not the specialty one she had at her place. Worry lanced through him, and he wondered if he should invest in a set for whenever she visited.

"Mmm, that is *good,*" Cassidy said, grinning at him once she swallowed her first mouthful. "Not bad for our last dinner together."

Well that was enough to knock him right out of his pondering. "Last dinner?"

"Yeah, you're pretty much back to normal and working, so I figure you want me out of your hair. Don't wanna smother you, after all."

Oh.

Right.

She was tending to him because he was sick, and that was over. Suddenly Mick realized that his copious access to Cassidy was about to reduce drastically and cold rushed through him.

"Are you okay? Do you not like it?"

"Huh?" He blinked, coming back to himself. "Oh, no, sorry.

I just got lost in thought." He picked up his own spoon and yeah, the stew *was* delicious. Warm, seasoned, and full of thick chunks of meat and potatoes. It was way richer than anything his nana had been able to afford when he was younger, which made sense considering the Millers were, well... *rich.* Funny how everything from soup to medical care benefited from being wealthy.

"This is great," he managed to say without letting bitterness seep into his tone.

"I'm glad you like it! You probably need all the protein, I figure."

"Probably."

They slipped into silence as they ate, and Mick grabbed one of the biscuits to fill his mouth and take away the obligation to dull the silence. That turned out to be a rather good idea, because the buttery yet subtle sweetness of the fluffy biscuit went perfectly with the salt and spice of the stew, making his whole belly feel warm.

Gosh, that was good. Way better than most of the lazy bachelor food he made himself. Maybe he could ask her to give him some lessons?

Or maybe he should let her concentrate on her health first.

Right.

Far too soon, their bowls were empty, and they were both just looking at each other. Mick wished he weren't so awkward, but he couldn't summon up anything to say. Because if he said anything, he was afraid the moment was burst, and she'd be out the door.

He was being silly; he knew that. He would see Cassidy nearly every day at work, and he could eat lunch with her whenever he wanted without anyone batting an eye.

But dinners... well, dinners were another matter entirely.

"You know, I'm really glad you came here."

Mick almost startled at Cassidy's sudden comment, not sure he heard her right. "I haven't done anything but cost you time and effort so far," he objected automatically. He didn't know *why* he said that, but it was just how he felt, apparently.

But it seemed Cassidy was willing to argue it. "What are you talking about? Because of you taking over my chores, Clara and Charlie have their free time back and are doing all sorts of projects to help people. And you make *me* feel better because, even though I'm not physically doing the work, it's kind of like you're my chore-avatar."

"Chore avatar?" he repeated, feeling his lips curl despite his objection. "That's a new one."

"Well, you know what I mean."

His curl turned into a full-blown smile. "I suppose I do."

"Anyway, stop trying to distract me. I'm glad you're here, and I'm glad that I could be there for you."

"I'm immensely in your debt."

But she just waved her hand. "Oh no, don't say that. Cause if you're in my debt, then I'm buried under so many IOUs from my accident that I'll never see the light of day again."

She did have a point there. "Alright. But I am immensely grateful."

"I know, Mick. You don't seem like the type to take anything for granted."

"Mostly because I'm not."

She nodded, grinning brightly at him. "So, how about we toast? It's a Ginger Ale toast, but I hear that makes it even more likely to happen."

"Ginger Ale does have a whole lot of magical properties according to my nana."

"Your nana sounds like a smart woman."

"She was, she really was."

"Well, to her memory, and to you," Cassidy said, raising her cup. "To your recovery and mine. To the ranch, my family and everything else in between."

Mick raised his glass too, clinking their edges together. "To all of that and more," he agreed.

They both drank up and sank into idle conversation all the way until a shrill alarm sounded. Cassidy let out a sharp curse and pulled her phone out, looking at it with surprise.

"Oh man, I didn't realize so much time had passed!"

Mick knew what that sentence meant. "You already booked for this evening?"

"Yeah, Clara and I have the final touches with the organization of the fundraiser with the church. I gotta boogey out."

He didn't want her to leave. He really didn't. But he couldn't beg her to stay and talk with him when she had more important things to do. "Thank you again," he murmured instead. "For everything."

"Anytime, Mick. You know I'm around."

Oh yes. He was acutely aware of that particular fact.

But then Cassidy was heading out the door and he heard her moped taking off. And just like that, he was alone again.

As the days passed and his endurance built back up, Mick found himself putting his everything into his work, feeling more invested in the Miller Ranch than ever. It wasn't just some temporary position to him anymore, and he didn't know what to do with that feeling, but he figured it would be a waste of time to fight it.

Besides, he was much more concerned with the fact that he

was suddenly very aware of Cassidy's every move. She still occasionally attended his work with him, but she usually ended up giving him fewer directions and more just talking. And perhaps the strangest thing was that Mick talked *back.*

Sure, he wasn't suddenly some chatterbox with a penchant for monologues, but he didn't go hours with just nodding or grunting. He *wanted* to talk to Cassidy. To learn about her life and hear her funny stories. He wanted to answer her questions and let her know he enjoyed her company.

Which was... strange. Certainly not something he'd encountered before.

But as strange as it was, it was also nice, and he liked seeing who Cassidy was when her walls were down. Not that he could blame her for having them; goodness knew he had enough of his own. He figured the same way some people had expectations about him as a black man, there were also societal pressures towards her as a woman, and as a disabled person. Even if that disability was most likely temporary.

Time began to flow quickly, and before Mick knew it, summer was beginning to wrap up and, while he'd taken to having lunches at the Miller's house, he and Cassidy were still circling each other with a strange sort of intensity.

And his RV was still lonely every night.

Several times he thought about asking her to dinner, just like old times, but the words always died on his tongue. She was his employer, for one. And secondly, she was just a genuinely kind person and he had no right to assume anything just because she'd helped him. In fact, the thought that he might possibly make her uncomfortable by asking her to his trailer under non-emergency reasons made him want to sew his own mouth shut.

So he stayed quiet, he worked hard, and he enjoyed the

days that Cassidy did spend with him. After all, the only times she didn't were when she had physical therapy or doctor visits.

But it was on a regular old Wednesday when he was surprised by Cassidy waiting for him on the usual path he walked to get to the main part of their little ranch.

"Mornin' Mick," she said, smiling at him from where she was perched on her specialty moped.

"Good Mornin'. What are you doing out here?" Had she meant to visit him? He might hope that was a 'yes,' but it was far too early for anything like that.

"Can I talk to you in the main house?"

Mick fought not to let his shock show on his face. Casual, *casual*. "Uh, is something up?"

"Let's talk about it once we're there."

...that was ominous.

"Don't worry, it's nothing bad."

That didn't make it any better.

"Alright then, lead the way."

He tried to remain calm as they walked along, but his mind was spinning. Had he done something wrong? Did they want him to move on? Were they going to work on expansion? Downsizing!? There was practically an unlimited amount of possibilities, but most of them were not what he wanted.

Actually... what did he want?

That question blindsided him, and he found himself internally speechless as his mind tried to come up with an answer. It was something he'd never really thought before, usually busy trying to either earn money or find a gig to live off of for a while. But shouldn't he have something beyond that? Some sort of... end goal?

"So, as you know, the end of your contract has already passed."

Mick started, not having realized that they'd reached the main house and were settled in the living room again. "It has?"

"I would tease you for not realizing so much time has passed, but I was surprised when I realized it too."

So that was it. His time with the Millers was over. He didn't think he'd ever find such a unique situation again, and just about everything in him protested at the idea of never seeing Cassidy again.

He still owed her, after all, and Mick didn't like living with unpaid debts.

What would he do? Where would he go? He had built his nest egg up again and could wander for maybe even a year.

...but he didn't want to.

"Anyway," Cassidy continued. "I'm sure you've noticed that my recovery is going slower than I would like."

That was true. Although he saw her walking more often and staying up for longer, she would still often be immobile after a physical therapy session, and sometimes her hands would curl up and shake so bad that she couldn't even open something as simple as a water bottle.

Mick hated seeing her like that, but he never commented. He knew better.

"I mean, I'm making progress every day, but I'm nowhere near being able to do all of my chores."

He agreed with her, but Mick only nodded, not sure where she was going with everything.

"So, although your contract was only for three months, I was hoping you might be willing to stay all the way until winter. Harvest season is always a wild time, and I don't want my family to suffer because of, well, you know."

Oh.

Oh.

They didn't want him to leave.

Cassidy didn't want him to leave!

It took a whole lot of control not to have his relief and elation show across his face, and Mick tried to cover it with a cough into his fist. But on the inside, he was practically jelly.

Winter was a full season away. That meant another season with Cassidy and another season to figure out the mess inside of him.

"I know that you wanted to continue west, but the work you've been doing for us is such a huge boon to my family. I know it's not actually *me* doing the tasks when we work together, but it *feels* like I'm being productive and contributing, so that's what matters. Honestly, without you, I think I'd have gone crazy weeks ago."

Mick swallowed again, trying to force his mouth to make words again. It shouldn't be so hard, and yet they felt clunky and weighted.

But how could they not when Cassidy was sitting across from him casually talking about how much better he made her life. Mick had had a lot harder jobs on much bigger operations, he'd even been a lead hand, but none of them made him feel as *important* as Cassidy did with her admission.

He was making a difference. A real difference. Sure, it wasn't a purpose or a goal, but it did make him feel *good*.

And maybe, for the moment, that was enough.

"I could stick around."

"Really?" The way she lit up wasn't fair. He'd always known she was stunning, but there was something about seeing her unabashedly grin that made his stomach flip. He would have thought the organ was tired of all the acrobatics given his most recent illness, but apparently not. "I hope it's not because you feel obligated or anything like that."

Her smile remained the same, but there was the slightest tremble of uncertainty to her words.

"No, I want to." Pride was swelling in his chest and he may have had a goofy smile of his own on.

"Alright! Fantastic! Well, in that case, I'll have our lawyer change this all up and we'll initial, sign, and yattah, yattah once he gets back to me."

"Sounds good." That was an understatement, that was for sure.

"Well, with that out of the way, would you like some tea and leftover pulled pork? Or is it too early for BBQ?"

"It is *never* too early for good BBQ."

They stood up together and walked to the kitchen, as natural as anything else. Mick knew he was still wearing a besotted grin, but he couldn't bring himself to care. He was just too happy that he didn't have to move on just yet.

Because, while there were a lot of things that were confusing him lately, he knew without a doubt that he wasn't ready to go.

20

Cassidy

*W*orking with Mick was quickly turning into the
best parts of her day.

Something had shifted between them ever since his sickness, something elusive that she didn't have a name for. But
whatever it was, it made him more open with her, and soon it
was almost like they were friends.

They'd developed a routine with work, that was for sure.
He hadn't really needed her there instructing him for a long
time, but he didn't protest. Usually they sank into idle conversation, and it flowed more smoothly than it ever had pre-
sickness.

They even started to occasionally meet up outside of necessary hours by having lunches and occasional afternoon snacks
together, whereas Mick had always done his best to avoid the

house before. It was a nice change, and one that Cass cherished more than he knew.

But, perhaps most importantly of all, she didn't have to worry about him leaving. She knew that he had to, eventually. Mick had made it clear that he was a nomad by nature. But she had him for at least a few more months, and hopefully that would give her time to dissolve the knot in her chest.

Because sure, she'd been attracted to other people in her life, but eventually that attraction would fade as she grew used to someone's face. All she needed was some time and then she wouldn't feel like the ground was falling out from under her whenever she looked at Mick.

"Catch!"

Cass reached her hand up to snatch the frisbee out of the air that Savannah had thrown her way. She was in her chair, resting for a bit before switching back to her walker. Charity wasn't exactly thrilled by it, but Alejandro had said playing would actually be a good form of physical therapy for Cass.

It was a far improvement from when she'd nearly passed out just about four months earlier, and proof that she was indeed getting better.

Sure, it wasn't enough, not nearly enough, but at least it was *something*.

"Toss it back and try not to make it swerve right this time!"

"Hey, less critique from the peanut gallery."

"What's a peanut gallery? Is that another old people thing?"

"Old people!" Cass let out a huff, although she was smiling on the inside. Savannah was as snarky as ever and had somehow grown another inch. What was Alejandro feeding the girl!? "You're lucky I like you, because otherwise I might bean you right in the face with this!"

"Pfft, like you could actually hit it."

"Alright, that's it!"

Cass put the frisbee in her lap and wheeled toward Savannah furiously, letting out a comically over the top yell. The young girl screeched a laugh and pretended to run away in slow motion, allowing Cass to catch up to her and grab her.

"That'll teach you!" Cass cried, tugging Savannah into her lap where the young girl flailed and kicked, jokingly declaring to unhand her. It was over-dramatic and fun and the perfect example of one of the reasons Cass loved having Savannah around.

"Well, well, well, did I hear the cries of a damsel in distress?"

Cass was actually surprised at the sound of Mick's voice enough to completely freeze, and Savannah sat up suddenly.

"There ain't no damsel here."

There was a pause, and then that low chuckle from Mick that she liked so much. "Oh, you're right. I didn't wear my glasses today."

"Well maybe you should ha—*oh my gosh*, your horse is *huge!!!*"

Finally, Cass turned around so that she could face the ranch hand directly and Savannah didn't have to crane to look over her shoulder.

"Hey," Cassidy murmured, giving him a quick wave.

"Hey there," he answered back, giving her the most subtle smile that somehow felt like it was just for her. Obviously that couldn't be true, but still, that was how it felt.

"*Hey*, why is no one answering about the giant horse?" Savannah leaped up out of Cass's lap and rushed toward the creature. "I've never seen one so big! Is he a giant? Is there a *breed* of giant horses?"

"He's a draft horse, actually," Mick answered, warmth in his voice. Cass watched with interest, noting that the ranch hand wasn't as taciturn as he normally was with people. Maybe he had a soft spot for kids? "They're not usually rode around on. They usually pull wagons or things like that."

"Whoa! Can I pet him? My dad says that I always need to ask before I pet something, for both my safety and the pet's. Is a horse a pet? It's kind of a pet, right?"

There was that chuckle again. "Yeah, you can pet him. Just approach him from the side and stroke his cheek. Don't put your hand right in front of him, because he usually thinks he's getting a treat when that happens."

"And he might bite me?"

"Yeah, he could nip you if you did that. But as long as you do as I said, he won't. Othello loves showing off to people, especially if they call him handsome."

"Well, if I looked like him, I'd probably be vain too," Savannah said, approaching him with respectful caution.

Honestly, Cass was impressed. Savannah was full of boundless energy and didn't so much walk places as she bounced, cartwheeled and skipped. But it was only with calm, relaxed energy that she approached Othello, lifting her arm smoothly.

"Hello, Mr. Handsome Giant Horse Sir, it's nice to meet you. You are one stunning creature."

It was adorable, there was no other word for it, but the cuteness of the moment increased tenfold as Othello practically shoved his face into Savannah's hand, nickering happily.

"Oh, he likes you," Mick remarked with a smile.

"Of course, he likes me. I have a sparkling personality and animals can tell that."

That was the breaking point and Cass erupted with

unchecked laughter. Oh Savannah. She certainly did have a way about her.

But Mick was as smooth as ever, nodding along casually. "Exactly. It's well known that animals are excellent judges of character."

"Exactly! You get it, Mr. Cowboy Man."

"Uh, you can call me Mick?"

"Like Mickey, the mouse?"

Finally, Mick lost his effortless cool, seeming to choke on his own sputter. "Would you believe I've never heard that before?" he asked when he could speak again.

"Absolutely not," Savannah answered without missing a beat.

And that had *both* of them laughing, Cass nearly tumbling out of her chair. It shouldn't have been that funny, it definitely shouldn't have, and yet something about her delivery and the look in Othello's dark eyes made the whole moment perfectly timed.

Eventually, when Cass could breathe again, she was just about ready to melt into her chair. Something about laughing made her feel particularly boneless, but in the best way possible.

"What's so funny?" Savannah asked flatly.

And then they were laughing again.

The second time they cooled down, Savannah just rolled her eyes. "Well, Mr. Cowboy, would you like to play frisbee with us?"

Mick's gaze flicked to Cass, and she tried to collect herself. Man, it was embarrassing to be wiped out by something as simple as laughing. There had been a time when she used to run a mile or two without being too bothered by it.

For *fun*.

"You know what? I was kind of fixing to stretch my legs. If you'd go on a walk with me, I'll let you hold Othello's reins."

Savannah's eyes nearly bugged out at that. "Are you saying you'll let me walk your horse?"

"I mean, it's not really walking h—actually. Yes. I will let you walk my horse."

"Deal!"

Cass knew what he was doing, and that he was about to walk over to her and offer to push her chair, but before she could protest, his gaze flicked to her and he gave her a quick wink.

There were certain things that were fair in life, but Mick winking at her was nowhere on that list. Suddenly her cheeks flushed and she felt a particular sort of warmth shoot through her.

Goodness. That man had a set of thick lashes on those onyx eyes of his. Lashes that she was utterly unprepared for. He should have to register his winks as weapons for their sheer power alone.

"You wouldn't mind if I gave you a push, would you?"

Any other person at any other time, she would have said no. But something about the way he tilted his head and his subtle, oh so subtle grin, made it impossible to do so.

"Sure, why not?"

And that was how the three of them plus Othello ended up along one of the slight trails across the property. The only talking was Savannah to the grand horse for a while, but eventually Cass got her wits together enough to say something.

"So what's the story with you and the big guy?"

"Does there have to be a story?" Mick responded with that vaguely wry tone of his.

"You telling me there isn't?"

"...no."

"Oh! I wanna know the story of how you met Othello!" Savannah chimed in, starting to jump up and down but catching herself after one hop and then clearing her throat. "Please?"

Mick paused for a moment, and Cass was sure that he was going to say no. But then, he started talking. Slowly at first, with his usual careful sort of cadence. But the longer he went on, the more he started to pick up speed, that honey-warm undertone to his voice becoming more and more audible.

"Well, when I was younger, I was real sick. Because of that, I got to go into this program that had kids like me work with animals. Eventually I got better, but I was hooked on all of it and I managed to get a summer job at a farm outside of the city. Took me two buses and then a four-mile bike ride to where they would pick me up, but I loved it."

"And that's where you met the horsie?"

"And that's where I met the horsie. He was a rescue, barely two years old and already massive. They were trying to tame him, but he was bitin' mad. I was the only one willing to feed him or rake out his stall."

"And he liked you?"

"Nah, the guy hated me."

Cass listened intently, her heart simmering with something that she couldn't identify. She'd always wondered what the backstory was between their ranch hand and his mount, but she'd always felt it was too private a thing to ask. Knowing that Mick trusted them enough to tell them... well, that was certainly a good feeling.

"What!?" Savannah gasped like it was the most shocking thing she'd ever heard. "He didn't like you?"

"Nope. He didn't like anyone, and I wasn't any exception.

He was mean. And he was smart too. He would find ways to mess with people that the other horses just didn't do."

"I don't get it. How did he go from that to being your horse? And why did you volunteer to be around him?"

"I don't know, to be honest. There was just... something in his eyes that made sense to me. He'd been dealt a bad hand and he was angry at the world, mad enough to try to take a bite out of anyone who tried to come close to him."

"Struck close to home?" Cass asked cautiously, tilting her head back to look up at his face. Mick returned her gaze, a slight flush to his unfairly clear skin.

"You could say something like that." He gave her a small, warm smile and *goodness,* it wasn't quite as bad as his wink, but it certainly packed a punch right to her heart. "And that's why, from the first moment he ripped a hole in my shirt, I knew he was going to be my horse."

"So they gave him to you?"

"Oh no. Hardly. I helped with his rehabilitation as best I could, being a teenage kid, and I worked there every single summer under the agreement that my wages would go towards buying the guy.

"The owners of the place tried to warn me against it. Said he could maybe be worked on enough to be non-violent but would never be a friendly companion. But I was determined. And you know, by the time I got out of my senior year, he finally warmed up to me and only me."

"And *then* you bought him?"

"Afraid not. It took me a whole 'nother year of working for them full time. Of course, I couldn't give them all of my wages anymore since I'd quit my afterschool job, so that certainly slowed things down."

Savannah frowned. "You had a job after school?"

"Yeah, nothing too fancy. Just worked at the local fast-food joint."

"But... why? Didn't you have homework?"

"I had homework."

Cass sensed that Savannah was about to say something particularly naive, but she went ahead and let the girl speak freely. The best way to learn something was to ask, after all.

"Were you bored?"

"I wish I had time to get bored."

"I don't understand. Why would you want to work at a burger place after school?"

Mick again didn't answer right away, and Cass knew she was staring at him, but she wanted to know what he would say. She wasn't so stuck in her own world that she didn't know *why* a teenager would need to work while going to school, but clearly Savannah—the daughter of a wealthy doctor from Cali —just didn't know about that side of the world yet.

"Well, because my nana needed the money. She got some benefits, but with those always being cut and her being sick, she had a hard time taking care of me. Besides, since she spent so long raising me, I figured I needed to repay the favor."

Ow. That stabbed into Cass's heart. "How old were you when you started?"

"Fifteen for the fast-food job. Of course, I mowed lawns and did newspapers before that. There were worse gigs."

"Benefits? I don't understand."

Cass took over, realizing it wasn't up to their ranch hand to explain economics and the unfairness of poorness to a kid. "Savannah, some people have more money than others. Mick's nana didn't have a lot, so he worked really hard to make sure they had enough to live."

"Oh... that doesn't seem right."

Cass and Mick exchanged a look and she desperately wished that she could tell what he was thinking.

Mick worked *so* hard. He'd basically almost had his brain fried by meningitis and yet he was back to the grind two weeks later. Insane. Yet he was incredibly poor compared to her own family. What had she done to be rich? Nothing. Just lucked out being born in the right place at the right time. It all seemed so very unfair when she thought about it.

"There's a lot about the world that isn't right," Cass answered softly.

"Huh. Well, maybe when I'm a grown-up, I'll fix it."

"If anyone could do it, it's you."

Savannah beamed at her, and Cass shot the expression right back. She wasn't the girl's auntie yet, but she certainly felt that way, and she couldn't be happier about her little pseudo-niece. "Thanks. I'll remember that."

"You better."

The conversation lulled as they walked along, Othello whinnying to demand more attention on him. Cass lasted maybe about another twenty minutes or so before she felt her face starting to overheat and her body scream at her that it wanted her to lay down. She kind of wanted to go back to the manor to rest, but she thought it would be in poor taste to leave Savannah alone with Mick, and Charity was still finishing something up in her garage.

But the idea of cutting off Savannah's time with Othello also seemed like something she didn't want, so she heaved a sigh of relief when she saw Charity walking towards them in the distance.

"Hey, I'm going to head in and make us some iced tea. I'll be back."

"Oh, do you want me to push you?"

"No, I got this part. Just remember to grab my walker when you circle back, if you don't mind. We're a lot closer to the house now than we were when we were playing frisbee."

"Alright. Whatever you need."

Whatever she needed? Goodness, coming from Mick's lips, that was a phrase that probably would have turned her knees to jelly if she didn't feel like she was on the verge of being painfully overheated.

"Thanks, Mick. I'll be back before you know it."

21

Mick

The Savannah girl was exhausting, but she was so earnest and excited about life that he told her everything she wanted to know, even about growing up in the city. It was the most he'd talked in ages, even with all the conversations he'd been having with Cassidy, and his throat was beginning to hurt by the time they were on their third circle. He looked to Charity a couple of times, begging for mercy with his eyes, and the eldest would chuckle and take over for at least a few minutes.

But as time continued to pass, it began to feel like Cassidy was gone for an awfully long while. He knew that she had to do some special maneuvering to get around the kitchen and haul tea to them, but... something just seemed amiss.

"Shouldn't Cassidy be back by now?" he asked her sister.

Charity looked up from the grasshopper she was showing

Savannah. "Hmm, she's probably just taking a nap. I've discovered lately that 'I'm going to make tea' is code that she needs to lie down."

"Ah..."

He lasted maybe five minutes more before the feeling became absolutely overwhelming, making the hair on the back of his neck stand on end. He couldn't help but remember the last time he caught her napping, where she'd rolled right off of the couch and ended up laying in a puddle. "I think I'm going to go check on her."

"Alright, would you mind grabbing me an orange while you're in there?"

"Sure, I can do that."

"Oh! And I want an apple pretty please!"

"Yes, Miss Savannah."

"Oooh, *Miss* Savannah. I like that."

"Goodness, don't you start," Charity said with a laugh.

Maybe Mick would have if he wasn't already walking away, mind on Cassidy and why she was taking so long.

He jogged to the manor of theirs, not caring that sweat was beginning to collect along his brow, but when he went inside, Cassidy wasn't on the couch.

Alright. Alright, don't panic. She could just be upstairs. Yeah, that was right. Mick knew that her room was on the second floor, and it would be entirely normal to pass out for a nap in her own bed.

If she was asleep, she probably wouldn't want to wake up. But... maybe she wouldn't be too mad if he called her.

Stomach twisting with a sense of dread that made absolutely no sense, he pulled out his phone and dialed her number. Chewing his lip, he waited for it to ring, only for it to go straight to her voice mail.

That couldn't be good, right? His gut was telling him that it couldn't be good.

Without a moment's hesitation, he whirled on his heel and ran right back out, sprinting towards where he'd left Charity and Savannah.

"Whoa, are you—"

"Cassidy isn't in the living room and her phone is dead. I realize it might be nothing, but—"

"No, no, that's weird. Savannah, you walk this guy to the stables. Mr. Mick, you come with me."

The two of them rushed right back, and Mick was practically pouring sweat, but he didn't care. He didn't even think as he followed Charity's sprint up the stairs, but she didn't stop him either. And yet, when he burst into what had to be Cassidy's room after the eldest sister, he wasn't prepared for it to be empty.

Cassidy wasn't there either.

"Where on earth could she be?" Charity said, her voice picking up to an octave Mick had never heard before. That was followed by a swear word and he'd never heard a single one of the Millers swear, so that let him know just how terrified she was.

"How much of the house is accessible to her?"

Before Charity could answer, Savannah was crying out for them downstairs.

"Geez, what now!?"

Although Mick wanted to stay behind and somehow look for Cassidy, he still went with Charity. It turned out Savannah was standing below the special lift, cupping her hands around her mouth to amplify her voice.

"Hey, there's a single sport drink on the counter, but none

in the fridge. Do you think maybe she went to get more? Where do y'all keep those?"

Wow. That was one heck of a conclusion. Cassidy hadn't been kidding when she'd offhandedly mentioned how bright the girl was.

"Savannah, you're a genius!" Charity cried, bolting back toward the stairs. "The basement! We keep them in the basement!"

Mick didn't need a mirror to know that all the color drained from his face. The *basement*? That had to be one of the worst possible options.

It was as a herd that the three of them raced through the kitchen and to a very solid door all the way in the corner. It was Charity who reached it first, and she threw it open before lunging forward to flick on the light. Thankfully, the bulb wasn't blown, because the stairwell was filled with an impressively bright light almost immediately.

And then Charity screamed.

22

Cassidy

Finally, Cass saw a flicker of light. It was a bit harsh, but nowhere nearly as extreme as the shrill scream that followed it.

Whoops, she hadn't thought about how she might be a frightful sight.

Oh well.

"It's about time you found me," she said with a weary sigh from the bottom of the stairs.

The trio at the top of the stairs thundered down to her, all of them talking at once. Before they could reach her, Cass made sure to call for them to stop. And impressively, they did.

"Sorry, I just wanted to tell y'all that you shouldn't move me. My back hurts, my chest hurts, and my head hurts. We'd best trust this to the professionals."

"Oh my gosh, Cass, oh my *gosh*," Charity said, her voice somewhere between whispered and wobbling.

It wasn't a sound that Cass liked to hear. It reminded her far too much of how her sister had screamed into her phone the night of the accident. But fortunately, it didn't last long, because then Charity was calling 911.

It was Mick who came down all the way to the bottom of the stairs, kneeling next to her. "Can... can I touch you, as long as I don't move you?"

It sure was a vague question, but Cass found herself agreeing anyway. "Sure."

Gently, oh so gently, his large hand reached out, gently stroking her damp bangs out of her face. When had her bangs gotten so long? Goodness, time just kept on marching, didn't it?

"What happened? You're being awful calm about this."

"Well, I kinda got tired of the whole panicking thing in the first ten minutes."

The corner of those full lips of his pulled down and Cass realized it probably wasn't the best time to joke around. That was a shame; humor was her best coping mechanism.

"Well, I came down here to grab a few bottles because the tea pitcher was empty and I've been sweating too much for water. I grabbed an armful—cause I'm not crazy enough to think I can carry a whole case, give me some credit—then I started to come back up. Carefully, mind you. I really *was* being cautious, holding onto the railing with a death grip and everything."

But Mick wasn't angry, just concerned, and that worry was written into the lines and slopes of his face. "Did you slip?"

"I wish it was something as simple as that. It's embarrassing, really." She trailed off, but when Mick didn't say anything else, she sighed and kept on. "A spider ran across my hand that was clamped onto the railing and I momentarily freaked out. Totally flung myself backward and, well, here I am. Completely forgot I was on the stairs, you know."

It was awful, yeah, and she was definitely in pain, but there was also a subtle sort of humor to it.

"Anyway, my phone was in my back pocket, so that got smashed. I *did* move my arm to pull it out, but that's all I've moved since I landed." Unbidden, a laugh bubbled up from her. "At least the spider was nice enough to leave me alone."

"You... you are an amazing woman."

"What, for falling down the stairs? I'm not even scared of spiders! It just startled me really badly."

But Mick just shook his head, still gently brushing her hair out of her face. "Absolutely amazing."

Flushing, Cass forgot her pain and just let him continue stroking her face. Moments later, Charity was on her other side, telling her that the ambulance was on its way. At least telling her and Savannah the story was enough to distract Cass for a while longer.

She stayed conscious the entire time, however, never going even close to that knife-thin slice of reality that lingered around oblivion. She tried to keep everything light, tried to joke, especially with Savannah, who was whiter than a sheet of paper—something that was pretty impressive for a tanned Latina girl.

But by about the third time she'd winced after trying to laugh, Mick leaned in, giving her a *very* particular look.

"What?" Cass found herself asking.

"It's alright to be angry. You've earned it. You don't have to pretend everything is okay for us."

Oh. That certainly hit home. Cass swallowed hard, and tears started to prick at her eyes. "I... I don't want to be inconvenient or make a scene." She paused. "Well, *more* of a scene."

"You do whatever you need to do to feel better."

The understanding in his dark eyes combined with the tenderness made her heart swell almost painfully. Why... why was everything he did just so intense?

She didn't know, and she didn't figure it out before the paramedics arrived, getting her up on one of their stiff boards. It was certainly an ordeal being hauled up the stairs, but Mick didn't break eye contact with her until the doors of the ambulance slammed closed behind her.

23

Cassidy

*I*n a blatant example of a miracle, nothing was broken and she didn't have a concussion.

Cass had been so sure that she'd reinjured herself, pushing herself farther back on her healing schedule, undoing months of work. But other than some gnarly bruises and superficial scrapes, she was alright.

Sure, she needed a couple good, long soaks in the tub with some Epsom salts, but other than that, she was right as rain.

Well, right as rain *physically*. Her mental state, however, was another story entirely. Because Cass was *angry*.

Not that being angry was new to her. Not at all. But the anger was so much different than before. Instead of being a suffocating, oppressive weight written into her broken bones, instead of making her want to sink into her mattress and snap

at anyone who dared disturb her, it was... well, it was invigo-
rating in a way.

That probably didn't make much sense, but Cass was at the
point that she didn't care. She was filled with a sort of determination she hadn't had before. One that wasn't tinged with
bitterness or resentment. She was going to get better, and that
was that.

It would be the ultimate revenge to all of the bad luck she'd
had in the past year. Because yes, life had been incredibly
unfair to her, but she also had plenty of advantages others
didn't. She had brilliant health insurance, and even if she
didn't, her family could probably foot even the most exorbitant
bill from the biggest, most expensive hospital in the world. It
was time to use those advantages and stop moping.

That was probably why, after a couple days' rest, Cass
rolled right up to Mick on a Monday morning, a thermos of tea
safely in her basket on the front of her altered moped.

"Hey there. It's good to see you," he stated with one of those
million dollar smiles on his face.

Good to see her? Cass tried not to stare at the ranch hand,
completely caught up in just... everything about him.

He was backlit by the sun, making his deep, dark skin glow
like he was something celestial. But even partially cast in
shadow, his features were striking and noble, those kind,
expressive eyes of his framed by impossibly thick and long
lashes. Goodness, he was stunning. She had no idea how he
walked around so humble and introverted, because he could
be a real heartbreaker if he wanted to.

"It's good to see you too."

And she wasn't lying. Her last image of him was how he'd
stared at her as she was loaded into the ambulance, expression
intense to the point of making her blush. Although she felt

that she'd become quite good at reading him, she hadn't been able to tell what he was thinking in those moments.

"What can I help you with?"

Cass didn't hesitate. Hesitation was for uncertainty, and although there were plenty of things in life she wasn't sure of, what she was planning to say wasn't one of those things.

"I'd like to have dinner with you."

That calm, effortless cool of his expression vanished, and the ranch hand blinked at her, clearly surprised. It wasn't exactly what she was hoping for, so she quickly kept speaking.

"You can say no, of course. And I won't get... weird about it. But I do have to say that I hope you won't." He was still staring. Goodness. People had told her that she could kind of have intense expressions sometimes, but clearly none of those people had ever had Mick turn his full gaze on them. "Because... because I think that we... uh, that there could be a chance for something great here between us, and I'd like the chance to see if that's so."

Oh no. His expression went from just plain surprised to completely blindsided. She'd ruined everything, hadn't she?

"Where... where is this all coming from?"

Where was it coming from? Had she imagined everything between them? The tension, the way he looked at her sometimes that made her feel like she occupied his whole mind? The hours and hours they spent talking, exchanging details, stories and opinions? Could she really have misinterpreted so much?

"Well, it's coming from us, I'd like to think." Perhaps being blunt would be the best strategy. "I'm attracted to you, Mick. You get me in a way no one outside of my family does, and I deserve a nice date with someone I like."

There, it was out there. He could say no. He could refuse

her. But she'd stopped being a coward and took hold of her own destiny. After all, she was a grown woman, and there was nothing wrong with her seeking out romantic companionship.

Except for the whole him being her employee thing and her controlling his livelihood.

... yeah, that part complicated things.

Mick said nothing for a long, long, *long* moment. It was hard to maintain eye contact, because with every passing second, she was so sure that he was going to say no.

But then, despite all of that, a slow and syrupy warm smile spread across his face.

"Yeah, I'd say you do."

"...I do what?"

"Deserve a date with someone you like. What day works best for you?"

Oh.

Well, that went better than she could have ever hoped for.

24

Cassidy

"Why are you smiling so hard?"

Cass looked up from her vanity, pulling out makeup she hadn't used in ages from the drawers. Charity was standing in her doorway, running a brush through her long, auburn hair.

"Do I need a reason to be happy?"

"No, I suppose not. But you're not the grinning type."

"I'm not?"

"No, that's definitely Clara. You usually just hum to yourself."

"I do not *hum*," Cass objected. Not that there was anything wrong with humming, but she was pretty sure she would know if that was something she did.

"No, you totally do. Haven't you noticed you haven't hummed since... well, you know."

Cass felt her smile diminish ever so slightly. "I guess I hadn't noticed."

"Right, well—"

Charity's rough segue was interrupted by the sound of the downstairs door closing and Clara calling up.

"Hello! Is anyone home?"

"We're up here!" Charity called, and honestly, Cass was relieved for the distraction.

It only took a couple of minutes before Clara showed up in the doorway, covered almost from head to toe in thick, viscous looking mud. And boy, did she *smell*.

"What happened to you?" Cass asked, her eyes going wide.

"I don't want to talk about it. Just know that our washer and dryer are going to be occupied for a while."

"Right..."

"Anyway, what's going on? You look happy and—*oh!* Is that the makeup I gave you?"

"Considering that you are the only person in our family who buys makeup... yes."

"Oh! Is there something special going on? Or are we dressing up for fun? OH! Are we having a tea party? It's been *ages* since we've had a tea party."

"Clara," Charity said with a wry grin. "We haven't had a tea party since we were teens."

"Yeah, like I said, *ages*." She stuck out her tongue, but her gaze was right back on Cass. "Come on, something is up, isn't it? Is it good? Please let it be good! I need it after the day I had."

"Well," Cass answered slowly. Part of her was hamming it up just to torment her sisters with the suspense, but another part of her was nervous to admit exactly what was going on. "I... just might have a date."

"A date!?" They said in unison like they were something out of a TV special.

"Hey, try not to sound so surprised."

"No, not surprised," Clara corrected, putting on what Charity unironically called her princess voice. "Just thrilled! This is wonderful, Cass! Getting out of the house and doing something just for you? I love it. Brilliant idea."

"Who is it?" Charity asked, ever the practical one.

Cass just shrugged, again not sure she wanted to admit it and potentially open that can of worms. Besides, she hadn't been on a date since before Charity's ex tried to extort their family, too afraid of that happening to her as well.

But she was almost certain that Mick would never, *ever* do anything like that. He was such a genuine, intense sort of man. He was kind to Savannah, not just polite, and he'd been so incredibly tender when she'd been hurt.

Then again... Eric had been good at first, too. He'd fooled them long enough for he and Charity to marry and be together for a couple years. And just look how *that* turned out.

"Maybe I can make the question easier," Charity said with that crooked smile she always wore whenever she thought that she was being clever. "Did Mick finally get the courage up to ask you, or are you the one who bit the bullet and took the leap?"

"Oh, Mick? Is that the gorgeous man I recruited from the grocery store?" Clara asked, clapping her hands. "Ah, I love it! I wish I got to interact with him more, but he's always been lovely every time we've eaten a meal together."

Cass sighed. She guessed there really were no secrets amongst siblings. "I asked him."

"Good job," Charity said, nodding. "What changed your mind on the whole no-dating thing?"

"I don't know if I've changed my mind entirely. I just know that I want to go to dinner with Mick, and that's all the reason I need."

"Exactly!" Clara was still clapping her hands, although she stopped when she realized she was getting little flecks of dried, stinky mud on the floor. "Oh dear."

"You should take a shower," Cass said, trying to get back to pulling out her makeup.

"What? No, not until I have more details. When is this date? Where are you going? Do you have an outfit in mind?"

"It's not until this Friday, and no to all of the above. I was just trying to see what I even have to give me ideas."

"...you shouldn't have said that," Charity said with a half groan.

"What, why?"

"Oh! This is perfect! I can help style you for your date!" Clara said, nearly clapping again and stopping just before she could send more detritus onto the floor.

"Right, because I have a real range of outfits between all my athletic wear and my lounging clothes."

Before the accident, Cass had a fairly decent wardrobe. But since, she'd lost so much weight and muscle that most of those clothes either hung on her like bags or slid off completely.

But Clara's eyes just lit up like it was Christmas. "You know... it's funny you should mention that."

"What do you mean?"

"Oh, you have no idea," Charity said with a knowing laugh. "Clara, you go get a shower. Cass, prepare to learn about a dozen new ways to say the word 'shirt.' As for me, well, I think I'm gonna go get snacks, because this is gonna be good."

25

Mick

$\mathcal{M}$ick stepped onto the first step of the Miller's wraparound porch, flowers in hand. He could tell by the trembling petals that he was shaking ever so slightly, but no matter how many times he internally scolded himself to calm down, his nerves were still jumping and jiving like they were at a real party.

Never in a million years had he thought he would be on a date with Cassidy Miller. He wasn't opposed to it, not by any means, but the more practical and cynical part of his mind wouldn't shut up about how it was a bad idea. She was his employer, after all, and if there was one thing his nana taught him about the world, it was never to mix business with pleasure. If there was a second one, it was definitely to never involve matters of the heart with the person who handed him his paycheck.

It was a huge potential mess in the making, one that could very well end with him being run out of town, and yet he kept on walking right up to their front door and giving it a knock.

It was crazy, really. Ill-advised, even. And yet, no one had ever been as kind to him as Cassidy. No one had ever made him feel so *seen*. And there was just something about her that he didn't quite have a name for, some unseen sort of magnetism that just drew him in.

"Coming!"

That was her. That was Cassidy's voice. Everything really was happening.

Technically, he supposed he should just turn around and walk away. But he knew he wasn't going to do it. The chance to say no had long since passed, flown right out the window when she'd first asked him.

But with the way she was staring up at him, so open and hopeful, he knew that he'd had to say yes. It had been like she would hand the moon and stars over for him to go on this date with her, and he'd never seen Cassidy so earnest, so willing to admit what she actually wanted. How could he ever punish her for that?

His internal circles were interrupted as Cassidy answered the door, dressed in a cute little retro number and even had her walker rhinestoned with a red ribbon on the top. She looked *gorgeous*. Her lips were a fuschia, while her eyes had been done in a dark liner that made them look even more intense than usual. He couldn't believe she'd done all that just for *him*.

"Hey there," she said, a crinkle in the corner of her eyes as she grinned at him. "Would you like to come in?"

"Of course." Mick stepped over the threshold, then held out her flowers before belatedly realizing that with both of her hands gripping her walker, she couldn't exactly take the bouquet. "These are for you."

"Oh, wow. When did you have time to find these?"

"I made time," Mick answered simply.

She laughed softly at that, letting go of her walker to take the flowers and bury her nose in them to take a deep breath. "Oh, these smell *great*," she murmured before putting them right into the small basket on the front of her walker. "Thank you, Mick."

"You're welcome."

If he was a more expressive person, he might have cringed at his own stilted response. But, as it were, he managed only a slight frown that Cassidy didn't comment on.

"I hope you're hungry. I might have gotten a bit carried away on the spread. Would you like to follow me?"

"It certainly would be strange if I didn't."

"True, but stranger things have happened."

Stranger things, like a rich, millionaire heiress being interested in her poor nomad of a ranch hand?

He didn't say that, of course, and instead nodded.

Smiling even more broadly, she led him to their dining area where indeed a plethora of food was laid out, almost to the point of overflowing. It was certainly impressive, but he found himself distracted by something else entirely.

"Where is everyone else?"

"Oh, out and about. Charity is at Alejandro's, Clara is with the lightning-struck farmer she's helping, Charlie is having a night in the city with his friends, and Papa is working on decorating the school gym with Savannah's favorite school librarian," Charity answered with a smile. "Some sort of Battle of the Books thing which sounds really fun, by the way." She chuckled, shaking her head at the thought. "Why, did you think when I asked you to dinner that I meant some sort of family affair?"

"I'm so used to at least someone else being here." The last time it had been just him and her in the house alone had been during her whole nap incident.

...which was also when those slender fingertips of hers had brushed against his chest. Was it strange that he still remembered that? He could recall every sensation and thought that had happened back then. It almost felt like a different lifetime.

"Well, I asked for privacy, and thankfully, they were all more than happy to oblige."

Oh? That was news to Mick.

"You told them about me?"

"Mick, you've worked here for months. They all 'know' about you. But if you mean 'did I tell them I asked you to dinner'? Well, yes. I did."

Mick didn't know why he was so surprised by that. Cassidy was an honest, straightforward sort of woman, so it made sense she would have been honest with her family. But still... he almost had expected to be some sort of shameful secret. Something she would want to hide from her rich siblings and father.

Huh.

Maybe he had some of his own biases to address.

But later, because then Cassidy was sitting and he followed her example, looking over all the delicious food laid out.

"Did you make all this?"

"Clara and Savannah helped me, actually. Then Charity, once Clara and I went upstairs to get ready."

Mick nodded, trying not to let the shock show on his face. She'd clearly gone through so much just to have a meal for him. It was honestly overwhelming.

"You didn't have to go to such lengths for me."

But Cassidy just shrugged. "I wanted to. And considering that I don't get to do most of the things I want to do, I'm not going to deny myself when I actually have the chance."

Well. He couldn't argue with that.

"I know it's not exactly traditional, but since I cooked, would it be alright if I served you? I want you to try certain things in a certain order."

"Of course. Whatever you want."

There was that grin again, making his heart thump. "You know, I feel like most people say that just to have something to say. But when *you* do it, it really seems like you mean it."

"That's because I do."

She flushed at that which made something in his chest swell, almost like a bird proudly preening. He liked that he so affected her, even though it didn't make sense that he did. He was a no one. No parents. No family. Just his giant horse and his camper.

Despite her flush, Cassidy lifted his plate and began to pile things onto it. Mick hardly paid attention to the food, watching her as she concentrated. Sometimes, he had a hard time believing she was real. He'd had a hard time connecting with people other than his nana ever since he was young and stuck in the hospital, being told by doctors that they had to cut his chest open. But there was something so... easy about talking to Cassidy. About being around her.

"Here you are!"

She handed him a *very* full plate, which he set in front of him while she served herself up. She didn't get quite as much as she'd given him, but it was an impressive amount none-theless. Mick always felt uncomfortable when women around him felt like they couldn't eat their fill, and he knew no matter what he told them, that they wouldn't really believe him.

It was a shame, really. Mick had met beautiful women of all sizes, but society sure did have a way of filling every single one of them with insecurities about their body. He was glad that he didn't have to deal with all of that, but just because it wasn't aimed at him didn't mean he liked it.

"So..." Cassidy said once they both had their plates in front of them.

"So..." Mick answered, mimicking her trail off.

She looked like she was going to say something, but then she stopped short, seemed to think a moment, then finally opened her mouth again. "Eat up! I definitely recommend dipping the biscuits in the chicken gravy and the mashed potatoes."

"That sounds easy enough," Mick said, internally chanting himself to just be normal for once. "Any other recommendations?"

"Yeah, eat the spiced peaches after the meat to reset your pallet. Oh!" Her eyes suddenly went wide. "I forgot the drinks!" She pointed to the two pitchers on the table, condensation all the way down the sides. "We have sweet tea, of course, and then water. There's wine in the fridge, but I didn't know if you drank or not."

"I do from time to time, but wine isn't usually my thing."

"Right, right, not really my thing either, but it seemed like the thing to do." She grinned again, her cheeks coloring. "By the way, I did look up recipes that were diabetic friendly. I'm sure I probably got some stuff wrong, but I did use sugar replacements for everything sweet and tried to focus on proteins and veggies."

"That's... very thoughtful of you."

That was putting it lightly.

People often had a very specific idea what diabetics looked

and acted like, and that idea wasn't really all that accurate. Especially for those with type 1 diabetes. Mick had had all sorts of problems when he was younger with maintaining his blood sugar. He'd get dizzy, or even occasionally pass out, until his nana sat him down on his bed and cried over how she was afraid she'd come home one day to news he was dead.

That had straightened him right out, but he still struggled occasionally, and the idea that Cassidy had made sure to make things that he could enjoy made the corners of his eyes burn. Which was insane. He was a grown man and he wasn't going to *cry* over a table full of food.

...at least not until he was in the comfort of his own RV.

"Well, I can't very well ask you to have dinner with me and not give you a dinner you can actually eat!"

"You'd be surprised."

"Maybe," she said with a cheeky sort of smirk. "People are pretty terrible."

"Now that, I agree with you on."

They shared a laugh and that seemed to break the tension between them, conversation beginning to flow more naturally. It helped that the food really was delicious, even if Mick ate slowly and carefully, occupied by all their talking as well as checking his glucose meter every once in a while.

"You know, I'm almost surprised you didn't show up with Othello," Cassidy joked when his plate was still half full. At least an hour passed and his food was long since cooled, but that didn't matter. "You two seem like such a package deal."

"Oh, we are." Mick grinned right back at her. "He is kind of a foodie and I wasn't sure the cuisine here would be up to his taste level."

"Ah, I see. And here I was hoping to impress him with my culinary skills."

"Trust me, you don't have to worry about impressing Othello at all."

"And why's that?"

"Because he trusts me, for some reason, and I've already vouched for you."

He didn't expect Cassidy to flush from her neck to her forehead, but she lit up a very pretty pink. "That's some pretty high praise there, I'm guessing."

"About the highest I can manage."

That flush grew brighter and the swelling in his chest grew even tighter, but not in a painful way. No, it was a floating, effervescent, thrilling sort of feeling that made him want to lift up off the earth and just let himself slowly drift up to the sky.

"You don't have to butter me up. I've already made you dinner."

"I don't know, maybe you deserve a little buttering up."

"You think so?"

He nodded, not trusting his words. And in an effort not to say anything else, he took a long drink of water. But even that reminded him of how she made sure he could have a beverage without sugar, and he felt a warmth rush through him again.

How different would his life be if he had met someone like Cassidy when he was a teen? Sure, he knew plenty of kind adults when he was a kid, but it seemed that once he was a teenager, all that kindness just kind of... dried up. He was always in the way or unwelcome or just on the outside. Never quite belonging.

But when Cassidy looked at him, when she laughed at his jokes or flushed at something he said, he felt like he actually was right where he was meant to be.

And that was a feeling he could easily get addicted to.

Conversation continued to flow, Mick once again talking

more than he normally did in a whole week before Cassidy. Before he knew it, there was a knock on the door and Mr. Miller was stepping in.

"Papa!" Cassidy said, clearly startled. "What are you doing back?"

"You told me it would be safe to come home at eleven. I did call, but you didn't answer."

"It's eleven o'clock!?"

Mick couldn't believe it. Eleven? They'd been talking and picking at their plates for four hours? That seemed utterly impossible. And yet, when he finally pulled out his brick of a cellphone, the screen did indeed say that it was eight minutes past the hour.

"That's insane..." Cassidy murmured.

"Right. Well, I see you're not done down here, darling, so I'll just head up to my room."

"Wait, have you eaten? Let me fix you a plate to take upstairs."

"Don't worry about it, I'll come help myself later. I slept in today, so I'll be up late."

"Alright then. Love you, Papa."

"Love you too, my Sundance Kid." Papa Miller did come forward to kiss his daughter on her cheek. Mick was surprised when the older man tipped his head to him, and he quickly nodded back.

"You have a good evening too, Mr. Jones."

"Thank you, sir."

"Please, call me Papa Miller. It's the only honorific that ever seemed to suit me."

Mick wanted to protest that he wasn't really a 'papa' kind of guy, but then the patriarch was walking up the stairs.

"Sundance Kid?" Mick asked, more than slightly curious.

"Come on, you don't get that reference?"

He just gave her a blank sort of look. "I'm afraid I don't."

Butch Cassidy and the Sundance Kid. I used to be obsessed with it when I was a kid, and my father certainly wasn't going to call me 'Butch,' ergo: Sundance Kid."

"That's... surprisingly adorable."

"Oh?" She sent him one of her snarky smiles, and he recognized that she was about to be cheeky with him. "You're saying you're surprised I'm capable of being adorable?"

"No, just surprised you'd admit to it of your own free will."

"Fair enough!" she said with a chuckle. "Not exactly something I aspire to."

"You don't have to aspire to be something you are naturally."

Her eyebrows went up at that and she didn't seem to know what to say. Apparently, Cassidy hadn't had many who called her cute to her face. That was a shame.

"Well," Cassidy said, her cheeks still pink. "I guess we should probably call it a night before everyone comes back. I know you're not the biggest fan of crowds."

He wasn't, and he was struck yet again by how much consideration Cassidy gave him. She didn't try to force him to do anything that made him uncomfortable, nor did she act like any of his idiosyncrasies were strange. Maybe that was why he was so comfortable talking to her. Most people either expected conversation from him as a form of social contract, or they would remark endlessly on how quiet he was—neither of which made him want to converse at all. But Cassidy never made him feel like that.

"No, I'm not. But I might tolerate a crowd if you were in it."

She ducked her head, one of her hands going to the back of her neck. "You don't mean that."

"I do." She looked like she didn't know what to say, so Mick decided to get her off the hot seat. Standing, he crossed to her and bent down to press a kiss to the cheek her father hadn't. "Thank you for everything. I've had a lovely night."

That was an understatement. Perhaps the biggest one he'd ever uttered. He felt more drawn to her than ever before, that biting loneliness that he'd been feeling every night faded into only warm happiness.

There was that beautiful flush, except this time he could see it going down her arms too. "Lovely enough to try it again?"

Funny, how such a strong woman sounded so vulnerable when opening herself to him. It still amazed him how much she lowered her walls for him sometimes and he still didn't understand why she found him worthy.

"I would be more than happy for a repeat experience." He gave her a wink, satisfied at the tiniest of gasps that left her lips, before turning to the door. But when he reached the exit, he paused, looking back at her for a long moment.

"Is there something on my face?" she murmured after a moment.

"No, I was just wondering. With this thing we've got going on, doesn't it mean that it's my turn to treat next time?"

"It means whatever we want it to mean. We don't owe anyone anything, except ourselves."

Huh, she really had a way with words, didn't she? Suddenly Cassidy seemed to be living for herself, and he wondered if her fall down the stairs had something to do with it.

"In that case, I'd very much like to take you out, Cassidy. To the nicest place in town."

The soft, sweet expression she gave him instantly burned itself into his memory. "It's a plan then."

26

Cassidy

One of Cassidy's biggest fears about their date was that it would make work awkward between them. After all, not only had she confessed to being both attracted and to liking Mick, but she'd had him alone in her house for hours, just her and him talking not about work, but only themselves.

However, by the time Monday rolled around and it was time to clear some thick brush on the southern edge of their land, she was ready to face the music and see if she'd ruined everything.

Naturally, she was quite pleased when Mick just tipped his head to her and asked if she was ready for another day of work.

And just like that, they fell into the same rhythm they always had, easy as everything.

It was *perfect*.

Outsiders would probably think it was strange that they

didn't talk about romance or their date at all during the week, but it made sense for them. The potential for... whatever it was they were doing was not something that should mix with the job, but rather something... private. Cherished. Something else that shouldn't be muddied with a paycheck.

But even though they didn't *talk* about it, it wasn't like they pretended it never happened. They sat together every lunch, and she let him push her chair when she wasn't in her moped. A couple of times, she even allowed him to hold her hand while she practiced walking without a mobility aid. They were closer than ever, but in the most comfortable way. Somehow, it felt like Cass had known him forever instead of just four short months.

"Hey, do you know why the tall, dark and handsome cowboy is standing on the porch with flowers?" Savannah asked, bounding into Cass's room with a popsicle in one hand and a wet-wipe in the other. The girl was notorious for getting incredibly upset whenever her fingers got sticky, so now it was a house rule that she always had to carry the two together.

"I'm sorry, what?"

"You know, the tall, dark an—"

"No, I know what you said, but since when do you know that phrase and also, since when do you think that boys aren't icky and are suddenly 'handsome'?"

"*Cass*," Savannah said, hands on her hips. "I'm basically a teenager now, thinking boys are icky is for kids. *Boys* are gross, but Mr. Cowboy is a *man*."

Cass could only blink at the child for a moment. "I... you know what, I'm going to have your dad handle that."

"Good luck. He just plugs his ears when I start to talk about hot actors on the TV."

It was difficult not to wince, but there was something

inherently wrong feeling about her little pseudo-niece calling anyone 'hot,' so Cass decided to just change the entire subject entirely. "So what does Mick want?"

"I dunno. He wouldn't tell me. Just said he wanted me to get you."

That was weird. Didn't sound like something Mick would do, but Savannah wasn't really one for making stuff up. "Alright, will you tell him I'll be down in a few minutes?"

"Okay!"

With that, Savannah scampered off, leaving Cass to wonder what Mick could want while she made her way downstairs. It did indeed take her a few minutes, and she almost expected some kind of prank. But sure enough, Mick was indeed standing there with another, even bigger bouquet of flowers.

"Good morning," she said, a curious expression on her face as she opened the door. "Is there a holiday going on that I'm not aware of?"

"Only if we want to make one," Mick said with a half-grin. Ever since she'd told him that whatever they were doing was whatever they wanted to make it, he'd run with the phrasing. She wasn't sure if it was because he wasn't used to thinking about what it was that he wanted, or if he was just happy that *she* was admitting what she wanted rather than denying herself from living because of her injuries, but either way... she kind of liked it.

"But actually, the reason I'm at your door at nine in the morning is because I would be honored if you would accompany me tonight to the one and only Mexican restaurant in town."

"You know, when you say it that way it sounds bad, but we only have two restaurants to choose from."

"It does make it easy to pick an option, I will admit." After a beat, that half-grin on his face faltered ever so slightly. "I understand if you're busy, or I didn't give you enough—"

"I'd love to!" Cass blurted out, her volume much louder than she meant it to be, startling both of them. Feeling her cheeks burn, she cleared her throat and tried again. "Do you have a time you'd like me to be ready?"

"I heard through the grapevine that the best time to head in is at seven. As a local, would you confirm that?"

"Yeah, that's usually when their live music comes in."

"Perfect. I'll see you then?"

"You'll see me then," Cass confirmed.

Mick looked furtively behind her, then from side to side, but before Cass could ask him why he was being strange, he suddenly leaned forward and pressed a kiss to her cheek. "I can't wait."

"Well, you're going to have to, because I'm not showing up in my pajamas."

For the first time since he'd arrived, Mick looked her fully over and a slow, heated grin passed across his features. It was a flirtatious look if she'd ever seen one, and it made her blood rush through her entire body at double-time. "If you did, I certainly wouldn't complain."

Cass looked herself over, trying to find what he was seeing to look at her like *that*, and it took several seconds to click. "... it's because I'm wearing shorts, isn't it?"

"It might be," he said, his grin growing bigger and his eyes going half-lidded. Goodness, a look like that needed a full-on warning. She was lucky she had her walker because her knees were *going*.

"So you're a leg man, Mick?"

"I think I might just be a Cassidy man."

"*Oh.*"

Not her most witty response, but she was too busy gulping to come up with a better one. A Cassidy man? That was... that was certainly something to think about.

But any thoughts she might have had disappeared when he leaned forward again and gently kissed her other cheek. When he straightened, she was sure her face was a bright red.

"Until then."

"Uh, yeah."

And then he was walking off, leaving her standing there in her doorway. When she finally came back to herself, she stumbled inside and rushed straight to her lift.

"*Clara!*" She called, trucking along as fast as she could. "Time for an emergency makeover!"

There was a thump, then the sound of heavy footfalls rapidly falling, then Clara was sliding out of her room into the hall, dressed in her retro nighty with curlers still in her hair. "What's the occasion? Destination? Are we doing formal, semi-casual? How much time do we have?"

"It's for seven tonight and Mick is taking me to La Cosina. I want something... pretty, but not too fancy."

"Semi-casual, warm color palette, second date. Got it. You go shower and I'll get everything ready."

"Right, okay!" Cass started to rush off but froze before she got too far. "Oh! Clara?"

"What, sis?"

"Can we put together something that shows off my legs?"

The smile on her sister's face was practically blinding. "I can definitely do that."

27

Cassidy

"Do I look alright?" Cass asked, running her hand through her short hair.

"Hey, don't mess with it. I just got the texture exactly right," Clara said. "This *really* accentuates your features. Think you're ever going to grow it out again?"

"No, I'll leave the mega-long hair to you and Charity."

"Can't say I blame you. This pixie-cut is just right for you."

Cass wryly thought back to how the whole thing happened. She'd been so mad that she couldn't brush her hair properly or plait it, that she'd cut it in the bathroom while crying furiously and cursing. Clara had found her after and fixed it up, but none of that entire experience had been very pleasant.

"It didn't exactly start off on the best note, but I'm pleased with where we are now."

"That's a good attitude. Now if only I could get someone else to think that way."

"Are you referring to that crotchety farmer guy you're helping?"

"I am indeed talking about that crotchety farmer guy I'm helping." Clara heaved a sigh. "I like helping him, I really do. But sometimes, he's just so angry with the world that it spills over and then he's angry at *me*."

"Doesn't sound very pleasant. Why don't you stop?" Cass knew Clara well enough to read her expression plain as day: her lips pressed together tightly. "You're not stopping because of me, right?"

Again, Clara didn't answer, and Cass placed a hand on her shoulder. "It's alright. I'm not angry. I... I get it. I was a real monster when I first came home too."

"I wouldn't say a *monster*. But there are some similarities, I suppose. And he *was* struck by lightning. I can see why he might feel that life's unfair."

"Yeah, it really puts my accident into perspective."

Clara nodded before taking a deep breath. "But enough of that. You're about to have a date with a charming man, and that's what you should be thinking about."

"Don't worry. I've been thinking about it nonstop since he arrived on our porch."

"That was rather romantic," Clara said with a sigh. "Like something out a movie. You'd almost be making me jealous if I wasn't so happy for you."

Cass sent her sister a warm grin. She had honestly thought that her family would have been more suspicious of Mick at first. Maybe it was pessimistic of her, but she'd kind of expected accusations of gold-digging or taking advantage. He was an employee after all, but so far everyone was wonderfully supportive.

She was grateful for it, that was for sure.

...she just wished her mother was around to give her input.

"Cass! Your gentleman caller is pulling up!"

That was Charlie, of course, and Cass rolled her eyes. Although he seemed to like Mick well enough, he also very clearly liked teasing his older sister better. Oh well. Little brothers: what else were they for other than to be pains in the bum?

"Coming!" Cass called before nodding to her sister. Clara then rolled her out and to the lift so she could conserve her energy, her walker folded up and strapped to the small rack at the back of her chair.

By the time they reached the front door, her stomach was churning with nerves. But it wasn't like she could bail at the last moment, so she opened the door and fixed what she hoped was a welcoming smile on her face.

"Hello there, Mick," she said softly as the man walked up the steps to their porch.

"Howdy."

It didn't make sense for something so simple to get her heart racing, and yet that was exactly what happened.

"Well, have a fun night, you two! I'll see you around midnight, Cass."

"See you then," Cass answered, giving her sister a nod before she hurried off.

"Ready for the best tacos in town?" Mick asked as soon as Clara left.

"They're the only tacos in town."

"Exactly."

Cass laughed, loud and bright to her own ears. "Alright, wheel me out."

He did exactly that. She had expected his camper to be waiting right outside sans his horse trailer, but instead he pushed her right up to Charity's truck.

"Wait, what's going on?" she asked.

"Your sister wasn't overly fond of you being able to get in and out of my camper, so she suggested I take her truck."

If Cass had more flair for the dramatic, her jaw would have dropped. Charity *never* let anybody else drive her truck. Ever.

Grabbing her wheels, Cass turned herself about and looked up toward Charity's room. Sure enough, her eldest sister was standing in her window, giving her a thumbs up.

Nosey.

But staring sister or not, Mick helped her into the truck, folded up her chair and put it in its special case in the back, then closed the door after her. He did it so seamlessly one would almost think he'd been doing it for years. Before she could even mention it, they were off.

It wasn't a long trip to the restaurant, just over ten minutes, and those minutes did indeed fly by quickly. Mick pulled up to the front, a gentleman as usual, helping her out of the car and wheeling her into the front waiting area before going to park.

He didn't leave her waiting long, so he must have found a great spot. It wasn't something that was always guaranteed in their small town, especially on a weekend, so luck definitely seemed to be on their side.

"Seems like we got here just in time," Mick said once he was inside, and the host instantly started walking them back to their table. "I thought there might be a wait."

"Sometimes there is," Cass said. "But you were smart in not coming on a Taco Tuesday."

"I'll keep that in mind."

They ended up at a table towards the middle of the restaurant, but there was enough space that her wheelchair wasn't in anyone's way. Quick as a flash, their waitress was at their table and asking for their drinks.

"So..." Cass began as they looked over the menu.

"So?" Mick asked, one of his thick eyebrows raised.

"What are you thinking of ordering?"

"Honestly, everything looks so good. You got any recommendations?"

"It's all delicious, to be honest, but I have a soft spot for their enchiladas. Charlie raves endlessly about their fajitas, though."

"Good to know."

"But what they're really known for here is their salsa. They have some *delicious* varieties here and free refills on all the chips."

"Free refills on chips? Be still my heart."

"Pretty sure you had surgery as a kid specifically to stop that from happening."

Mick froze, his recently delivered drink halfway to his mouth and his eyes going wide. For a split-second Cass thought that she'd gone too far, but then he let out the loudest, booming crack of laughter she'd ever heard.

Cass felt a couple people look at them, but she didn't care. Her whole concentration went to watching Mick laugh, his head tilted back and his chest expanding with the sheer force of his mirth. It was a wonderful, warm sight, and she wanted to memorize everything about it.

When he slowly wound down, there were tears in eyes from laughing so hard. It took him several moments and a long drink of water before he could look at her again and use full words.

"I wasn't expecting that," he gasped finely.

"Yeah, I put that together."

He laughed again and Cassidy found herself chuckling too. It was hard not to when he sounded so incredibly happy. And they kept right on randomly breaking into chuckles and giggles right up until their waitress came to take their entree orders and even a bit after. Really, it was only when their delicious food arrived that they sort of calmed down, but even then, there was an effervescent sort of levity to everything they said to each other.

It was good. It was *really* good. Better than Cass could have ever hoped. Unbidden, warm and fuzzies were flowing through her like a high school crush, and every time Mick looked at her, she swore she was going to break into giggles or melt into a puddle.

"So, not to be presumptuous, but I would say that this second date has been more than a success," Mick said when their plates were empty.

"I think I would more than agree," Cass answered, licking the last of her queso from her spoon.

"You think?"

"Well, there is such a thing as confirmation bias."

"Oh, so you're saying that you wanted this to be good then?"

"Well, I certainly didn't want it to go badly."

"Good to know. I'd hate to think you were stacking the deck against us."

The tension was cranking up between them with every new sentence, and Cass felt her heart racing. She wanted... she just wanted so *much*, and all of it had to do with the man sitting across from her.

For once, she decided to chance it and reached across the table, resting her hand over his. He looked at her a moment, his gaze utterly intense again, but after a moment he turned his own hand over and intertwined his fingers through hers.

They were quiet then, probably for the first time since their whole date started, just looking at each other. Cass couldn't remember a time where she felt so intensely drawn to someone, caught up in the gravity of everything he—

"So will we be wanting dessert this evening?"

They both practically jumped. Cass had never felt like telling a server to beat it before, but she did at this moment.

"Oh, um, I wouldn't mind the flan," Mick said before looking to Cass. "You want something, right?"

"Yeah, I'll take the cheesecake empanada."

"Perfect," their server said with a genuine smile, and Cass almost felt guilty for feeling irritated with her.

...almost.

"I'll be right back with that. And would either of you want a refill?"

They both ordered water and then they were back on their own. But the intense, meaningful minute between them was gone, leaving an awkward sort of reality where they were both staring at where their hands were joined.

"Mick..." she murmured, eventually, her tongue suddenly heavy in her mouth.

"Yeah?"

"Where are we going with this?"

"What do you mean?"

"Your contract is ending soon and you're going to leave. I'm not against enjoying time together while we have it, but... but I kind of want to know what your plans are. If you have any at all."

He blinked at her a moment, like that was the last thing he expected. How could he be surprised? She lived her life by schedules all the time, between her work, physical therapy, doctors' appointments in the city and everything else. Not to mention the natural sort of schedule that came from owning a small ranch.

"I'll admit I haven't quite thought about that. I didn't exactly expect all this, and, well, I just...don't know."

Cass drew in a deep breath. It wasn't some undying declaration of love, but she couldn't blame him. They were in real life, not some Soap Opera fantasy, and changing the entire course of his life just because of the intensity between them might not be a wise course of action.

But still, she wished that it could be simpler. Everything that was happening between them was so new to her, sparkling and shining with excitement, with uncertainty. She wanted to look at it every which way, examine it until there wasn't any more mystery, all while enjoying Mick's company.

Too bad things didn't work that way.

"I don't know either," she admitted finally.

Mick gave a grave nod, and suddenly the feeling was so much different than it had been just earlier. "So, for now, should we just... keep going until one of us knows?"

Cass didn't answer right away, truly thinking about what he said and all that meant. "I can't think of a better plan."

"Alright then," Mick said, squeezing her hand. "Like you said, we make this whatever we want it to be until we want different things."

"Sounds good to me."

Their desserts came and they sat quietly for a while enjoying the delicious flavors together. It was bittersweet, as real life so often was, and Cass somewhat enjoyed the melancholy of it. She could trust Mick to always be honest with her, even if his answers weren't exactly what she wanted. That was far more valuable to her than any sort of yes-man.

They took their time, but eventually their desserts were gone, and they'd sat an additional half-hour at the table. Cass mentioned they should leave, but Mick seemed reluctant to call an end to their night. Which, actually, was pretty flattering.

"Don't worry," she said with a grin, squeezing his hand once more. "I'll still be here tomorrow. And the day after. I can't exactly escape fast in this chair of mine."

"You say that like I haven't watched you book around with your walker."

"You overestimate my skill."

"No, I just know better than to underestimate your determination."

She flushed at that, she knew she did, but he didn't remark on it. After more banter, they readied to leave, Mick bringing her just outside, then walking off to pull up Charity's truck.

Cass hummed to herself as she waited, but then someone came out and lit up a cigar. Not entirely uncommon in her area, but the smoke irritated her somewhat sensitive lungs. Before the accident, that kind of stuff had never bothered her. She didn't know if it was all the surgeries or the fact that her body had gone through so much trauma, but it was one of the many inconvenient results of surviving something most people wouldn't have.

She wasn't about to reprimand someone for lighting up outside, however, so she wheeled to the side of the restaurant, happy as a clam. She was pretty sure that Mick would be able to spot her without too much—

A peal of mean, vicious laughter distracted her, such a distinct sound she knew it at the first tone. It was something she'd heard often in middle and high school, when Clara had been teased mercilessly for her weight. The girl had biceps the size of some of her peer's heads and yet she'd never do anything to defend herself, leaving the job to Cassidy. Charity would have done it if she hadn't already graduated, the age difference between her and Clara too wide for them to be in school together for long.

Wheeling closer to the side of the building, she just barely spotted what had to be a couple of wait staff smoking cigarettes with what looked to be a couple back-of-the-house employees. They were all standing in a circle, laughing among themselves.

Cass turned away, assuming it was just intrapersonal work drama that was none of her business, but then she heard one of the men speak.

"The Millers stick to themselves for years and suddenly we've had two in our restaurant on dates in one year. What does Guadalupe put in those tortillas of hers?"

Oh, huh. Cass hadn't thought about it, but he had a point. Their little family was pretty insular and had been ever since Ma had died. Sure, they had friends when they were younger, but as they grew older and most folks either went to college or moved to other places, most of the Miller children just associated with their siblings.

That probably wasn't healthy.

"I told you she's magic. Nothing else would get them to come out of their mansion."

There was another peal of laughter around them, and Cass wondered if she was wrong about the whole vicious thing. They just seemed like they were enjoying their break.

"So, do y'all wanna take bets on whether wheels hired that guy or if he's looking for a payout?"

Nope, there it was. Why had she doubted herself?

"Are you asking if you think she hired some dude escort or if he's a gold digger?" another said, and Cass could practically hear the condescension in her tone. Her fingers gripped her wheels harder, but she just sat here. Let them say whatever they wanted to say; it didn't matter.

"Uh, definitely a gold digger, I mean come on."

"Why do you say it like it's obvious?"

"It's obvious!" one of the men said, sounding surprised. "Escorts are supposed to be high class, you know, sophisticated types. Ghetto types like that are always looking for some sort of payout."

Suddenly Cass saw *red.*

"Don't you think it's weird how that other one is also dating that Latino doctor? It's like they don't like to date people of their own color."

That was too much. *Far* too much. Rage rushing through her, Cass rolled completely out from behind the corner and went straight for them.

"Believe it or not, in my family we judge people by their character and not the color of their skin. You should try it sometime, you bigot!"

The group froze, which was fine by Cass. It gave her time to say everything she needed to say while she wheeled towards them. "You think that you have any right to judge Mick? Or Alejandro? Or my sister? You know nothing about us."

She stopped her forward motion and gripped the wheels hard. "You would be lucky to be half the man that Mick is! To have even an ounce of his character or patience or kindness. So, you can all stand here in your little hate circle and insult people so you can feel superior for once in your miserable lives, but—"

A large hand on her shoulder distracted her, and Cass jerked to the side.

"May I take you home?"

Cass blinked at Mick, whose face was an impassive mask. He didn't even look at the circle of employees, instead focusing on only her.

Although he didn't have any expression, any outward sign of pain, Cass was just so *hurt* for him. She wanted to say something, anything to fix it, but nothing came out.

He continued since she was at a loss for words. "It's been a lovely night. Let's not waste any of it on people who don't deserve it."

He was so gracious, so much more forgiving than she was. But Cass couldn't let it completely lie. Glancing back over to the group, she pulled her lips back from her teeth in a snarl.

"I'm going to have a good talk with your owners tomorrow, so I'd spend the night thinking about what excuses you're going to try to make to save yourselves." Turning her gaze back to Mick, she nodded. "I'm ready."

They were quiet as he wheeled her to the truck, and still quiet when he helped her in. It would be a long drive home.

28

Mick

ick was quiet on the drive from the restaurant to the Miller Ranch. The dinner had been quite the rollercoaster and yet he hadn't wanted it to end. The thought of going back to his empty camper was unreasonably depressing, and he'd found himself trying to think of excuses of how to extend their night on the town.

But when he'd pulled up to the front of the restaurant, Cassidy hadn't been there. Concerned, he'd decided to get out and walk around the perimeter. He wasn't sure what he expected, but it certainly wasn't to see her halfway around a corner eavesdropping on a group of workers. He wasn't quite sure *why* she seemed so enraptured until he heard exactly what they were saying.

He couldn't say that he was surprised, but he was disappointed.

Mick had been living in the Miller bubble for so long that he'd almost forgotten how jarring it was when running into someone like... that. It hit him hard and he just stood there, staring for a long moment.

And then Cassidy had practically charged.

She'd been something, really something. A force of nature, an ardent defender, a beautiful justiciar as she completely reamed the group out.

It had touched him, of course, to hear her defend him so intensely. But also, it let him know exactly what she thought about him, because she clearly had zero idea that he was there.

The whole situation was wrong, though. She shouldn't have to defend him. And she was his boss. It wasn't right that he was putting her in that position. Having feelings so intense he could hardly breathe when she was around wasn't right, either.

They couldn't be a couple. He would bring nothing but trouble and drama to Cassidy, and to the entire Miller family.

And they didn't deserve that. They were good people.

"I'll pack up your chair and take you home," he said after he had her settled in the truck.

She gave him a flushed nod. "Thank you, Mick."

He shut her door for her once she was fully in, then did exactly what he said he would. And on the ride home, he was too embarrassed to say a word.

The drive was over and he parked in front of the Miller manor, then opened her door. He gently helped her into her wheelchair.

And so he pushed her up to her front door, taking his time on the wheelchair ramp to the porch, but he lingered just outside the entrance.

"I had a great time," Cassidy said softly, looking up at him with such a soft expression that he wanted to kiss her.

But he couldn't, could he? This relationship would go no further.

"So did I. You have a good night, and I'll see you for work on Monday."

"Actually, why don't you come over for lunch and tea tomorrow? I'm sure Savannah would love to walk Othello again."

Mick couldn't help but smile. She was so kind. There was something inside of him that was very afraid that she would get tired of him or come to her senses and realize she was pseudo-courting a no-account ranch hand from the big city. A cowboy with skin a different color than hers who would bring prejudice and difficulty into her life.

"Thank you, but I have a lot of chores to catch up on," he said, instead of the 'yes' that he wanted to say.

"Oh, okay," she murmured, looking up at him through her lashes, her eyes misty.

They looked to the now-open door to see Charlie standing there, holding it open for Cassidy.

"Good night," Cassidy said, then she rolled into the house.

"Goodbye," Mick said, too quietly for her to hear.

29

Mick

*L*ife on the ranch continued to march on, with Mick avoiding Cassidy, spending his time in his trailer or with Othello.

He would sit in his camper alone, staring at his phone or laptop while trying to distract himself from his loneliness. He knew he could just text Cassidy and ask if she wanted to go for a night picnic, or if there were leftovers at her place. But he told himself it was better if he stayed away.

He started getting his camper ready to head west. As soon as his contract was done, he'd leave. His heart was breaking and he really wanted to just get up and go, but he wasn't the type of man to break a contract.

Days became weeks, chores and tasks keeping him as busy as possible, harvest season kicking into full gear with a vengeance. There was always something to pick, process or prepare and Mick liked the busy schedule.

It was easy, it was wonderful, and the only real difficult part was seeing Cassidy in pain.

They hadn't discussed the night at the restaurant. Mick decided Cassidy must feel too embarrassed for him and was taking his clue to be strictly boss and contract worker. After that night, she must have been able to see that their relationship would never work. He still thought she was beautiful, smart, strong, and kind-hearted. His heart hurt whenever he had to see her because he wanted to hold her in his arms and kiss her soft lips. But that wasn't ever to be. "Hey, are you ready to go?"

Mick looked up from the book he was reading. He'd been given the task of driving Cassidy to her PT appointment instead of Charity that day. All the other Millers were busy. That wasn't what Mick really wanted to do, having to be so close to her in that enclosed truck. But he had agreed since he was a contract helper and Cassidy needed to get to her appointment.

"Yes, ma'am. Are you?"

Cassidy cringed. "All dressed up and ready for pain."

She was in her chair, which she was using less and less. She could definitely just go to the appointment with her walker, but they'd both learned that afterward she'd usually be too weak to get back into the house without her chair.

But Alejandro was very optimistic about her progress and said he was only able to work her so hard because she was doing brilliantly. Finally, she'd started to gain some weight, both muscle and fat, and Mick noticed Cassidy didn't always try to avoid her reflection all the time.

"You almost sound like you're looking forward to it," he remarked while they headed out the door.

"No, I dread it, to be honest. But what I do look forward to is how much stronger I feel after a few days and several warm baths. You know I haven't had my hand curl in over a week? And I can take the stairs almost all the time."

"You also can hold the drill without your fingers cramping," Mick offered, helping her into the truck even though she was quite capable of doing it herself.

"You noticed that?" she asked in surprise, her eyes going wide as she slammed the door shut.

But Mick just shrugged. He noticed a lot. In fact, he liked to think that he'd become a Cassidy expert. He knew how she liked her tea; he knew how she liked each of her chores to be done. He knew her expression when she was pushing herself far too hard, and he knew her expression when she was about to be overwhelmed by frustration. He knew so much about her and yet he still wanted to learn more. From afar. Without her knowing he was watching.

Physical therapy came and went, then it was a new day. Winter marched ever closer, with the end of his contract in just another month and a half. He didn't think he'd ever had time go so slowly.

And yet, as the days ticked down, Mick became more and more attuned to their passing. The Miller Ranch had started out as his place of employment where he lived on the fringe, to the closest that he had ever felt to home, to somewhere he had to leave or his heart would break. He kept waiting for that call he always felt that would inevitably tug him away, but it never happened. In fact, the very idea of leaving made him lay awake, staring at his ceiling in sleepless anxiety. This time, he would be heading west to escape his feelings, not from being drawn away.

Cassidy approached him while he was out at the ranch one day, grabbing some tools from the shed.

"You know, your contract is ending soon."

He'd expected to be surprised that the time had finally arrived for this conversation, but he just gave her a knowing shrug.

"I am aware."

"And?"

"And I think it's a good time to let that contract come to an end."

"Oh..."

Cassidy froze, trying to contain her emotions. She looked hurt, shocked even. But they had agreed that they would only be a thing as long as both of them wanted to be a thing, and she had to know he might head west someday.

Cassidy struggled to find her words, then finally said, "And why do you think that?"

"It's time to head west."

Cassidy frowned. "What happened, Mick? You seemed so happy here. We were so happy, I thought. And then..."

"You have a good thing goin' here with your family. But it's your family, not mine. I don't belong."

"We feel like you are part of the family," Cassidy said, her eyes pleading.

He looked away. "I'll just cause trouble and get in the way. You'll be strong enough to get back to work before you know it. It's best I leave now." He couldn't look in her eyes. She'd see the pain behind the tough-guy façade.

She hesitated. "Alright, then. Your contract ends at the end of the year. I'll make a list of the things for you to get done before you go." And she wheeled away.

Mick was sure that his heart had broken, right then and there.

30

Mick

$\mathcal{A}$ knock sounded on Mick's door, drawing him away from the Netflix series he was binging on. Saturday mornings belonged to him and Othello, so it was unusual for any of the Millers to come up to his door. Even Cassidy liked to sleep in, rolling in for 'lunch,' which was really more of a breakfast for her.

Making sure he was relatively decent, he answered the door only to see Cassidy on her little moped.

"Everything okay?"

She smiled up at him with that beautiful smile of hers, the corners of her eyes crinkling. "What, I can't visit my employee without something being wrong?"

"Right, uh, would you like to come in?" Huh. Even after living on the ranch for many months, he was still painfully awkward. He didn't know what they saw in him, but he was endlessly grateful for it.

"Oh, no, that's fine. I just swung by to formally invite you to Christmas cookie baking and decorating our tree."

Mick stared at her a moment, both amused and a little confused. He'd been on the road and by himself for so long that he hadn't really celebrated Christmas beyond having a special treat with Othello while watching a few classics on his laptop and eating way too much Chinese food. Christmas reminded him of the day his nana died.

But Cassidy seemed to take his pause poorly. "Of course, you don't have to. I realize I never even asked you if that was something you celebrate. If you—"

"I'd love to." Mick wasn't sure why he'd said that. Perhaps it was safe to spend time with the whole family around? He was leaving soon, after all.

Somehow, her already brilliant smile grew even more shining. "You will?"

"Yeah. When do you need me over?"

"Be at the house in an hour and a half wearing something you don't mind getting both flour and tinsel all over."

"How many cookies do you even have to bake?"

"Well, Clara is planning on making enough for the congregation tomorrow... and most of the town."

"Are you serious?"

Cassidy beamed at him as she nodded. "We take Christmas *very* seriously around here."

Mick let out a breath, wondering exactly what he had gotten himself into. "Thanks for the warning."

~

Cassidy hadn't been exaggerating.

Not even a little.

The first three full hours were spent with him and Charlie erecting the tree in the living room and then staying up on ladders while the girls told them where to hang the higher ornaments. It wasn't just the normal trio of women he was used to either, with Savannah and the youngest Miller—Cecelia—also there. Granted, the younger two mostly just ate snacks and joked around, with Savannah exclaiming that every new ornament was the cutest ornament yet.

It was fun though, as much as it was surprisingly intense. And then there was tossing a tightly wound ball of tinsel back and forth until the tree had a beautiful swirl of silver all the way down it.

The pine was truly massive, about ten feet tall plus the shining star they put on top. It was certainly the biggest that Mick had ever interacted with.

And yet, despite its staggering size, it wasn't gaudy. Maybe that was because it was covered in homemade ornaments and memories; maybe it was just because he had such a soft spot for the Millers and all their eccentricities.

By the time they actually rolled around to making the cookies, Mick's feet were sore and his stomach was rumbling. He didn't need to worry though, because he and Charlie were stationed at the kitchen island where they could sit on stools and munch on the grilled cheese sandwiches Clara made them. Mick had never known a grilled cheese to be a fully satisfying meal, but the woman did something to the sandwiches to make them incredibly filling.

"Alright, I'm going to head out now," Papa Miller said a few minutes after they were all done snacking. Cassidy's eyebrows shot up in surprise, which told Mick this wasn't a normal thing.

"You have plans?"

"Oh, didn't I tell you? I invited Mrs. Vagenacht over to join us. She doesn't have a vehicle since she lives in town, so I was going to pick her up."

"Mrs. Vagenacht, huh?" Charlie asked while waggling his eyebrows. "That's the pretty librarian lady you met at Alejandro's birthday party, right?"

"Whatever you're doing with your face right now, you need to stop it," Papa Miller said with a shrug.

"What are you talking about? This is just my face."

"Yeah, yeah. I'll be back in about thirty minutes, give or take."

There was a chorus of 'oohs' from the five children like something out of a sitcom, but Papa Miller just rolled his eyes.

"I feel like I'm missing something," Mick admitted.

"It's nothing," Cassidy said gently. "It's just nice to see Papa interact with someone besides us."

Ah. Mick got what she meant between the lines. How long had their father been a widower anyway? Clearly long enough for all of his children to be happy at the thought that maybe he was moving on.

It was Savannah who got the ball rolling again, setting a thick container of flour down on the counter with a bang.

"Is this what you wanted me to get from the pantry?"

"That it is," Clara said with a grin. "Alright, Mick and Charlie, you're on greasing pans, taking cookies out of the oven and putting them on the cooling rack, and washing dishes."

Mick gave a resolute nod. Those were all things that he could do.

It wasn't hard to sink into the rhythm of it once the girls got going, and somehow there was space enough for all of them in the large kitchen. It helped that Cici and Savannah were together at the counter, dutifully icing, glazing, or doing whatever it was that each cookie needed.

The whole kitchen smelled *delicious*, and there was so much going on that it was impossible to get bored. Between the carols playing, Clara doling out orders, Cassidy fetching drinks and Charity measuring out all the dry ingredients, there was always someone who needed help with something.

And yet, it wasn't hectic. There was a pleasant sort of warmth and cheeriness to the room. Just a bunch of people enjoying each other and doing something they all enjoyed. Perhaps it was kind of sad that the whole concept was so foreign to him.

Mick could faintly remember, back when he was young, his nana putting together the best she could for him. Some years he'd been too sick to help her, but she'd pull her threadbare, comfy recliner to the entrance of the kitchen and have him sit there while she worked.

He'd always treasured those times, truly, and he'd thought he'd lost that sort of comfort forever. Funny, to have found it almost all the way across the continent with a family that was the opposite of his own.

"Open wide!"

Mick did on instinct, his hands submerged in soapy water despite the incredibly nice dishwasher right beside him. A small, savory little morsel landed on his tongue, flavor exploding in his mouth.

"Do you like it?" Cassidy asked, grinning almost shyly at him. Considering how strong of a woman she was, he took that as a pretty high compliment that she cared about his opinion so deeply.

"I do. What was that?"

"A stuffed mushroom. I haven't made them in ages, but I made some last night because I couldn't sleep."

"Why couldn't you sleep?"

"No reason."

"Because she was scared to invite you to this thingie," Savannah offered happily, a dollop of icing on her nose.

"*Savannah!*" Cassidy hissed.

"*Cassidy,*" the young girl echoed. "See, I can do it too."

The two blew raspberries at each other, and Mick couldn't help it. He laughed. He laughed so hard that he had to grip the counter with his soapy hands lest he fall over.

"Careful," Clara warned. "Don't kill our guest now."

"Sorry, my gift of humor is truly a curse," Savannah said with a dramatic hand to her forehead. Unfortunately, that smeared icing there too and Cici declared it was time for both of them to wash their hands before round two.

Clara pointed at Charlie. "Hey, Charlie, I need to get more eggs, milk, flour and vanilla from the pantry. Can you help me carry all that since you've opted out of the dishwashing portion of this venture?"

"I hear your veiled jab and I can't even be mad," the brother said with a laugh from where he was playing with his phone by the counter. "My muscles are yours."

"Oh, such a generous gift."

The two of them headed off, leaving just Mick and Cassidy. The cowboy looked to her, watching her expressions as they flitted across her face. "Why were you scared to ask me?"

"Hmmm?"

"Savannah said you were scared to ask me to this. Why?"

"Oh, uh... well. You know, you're more of a solitary person, and sometimes my family can be too... much."

Oh Cassidy. Beautiful, fearless, loving Cassidy. Mick finally wiped his hands, pulling her into a hug.

"I'm glad you asked me. Really."

"Really? That's... that's good. I was just nervous because you hadn't mentioned Christmas at all."

"Probably because I'd forgotten it was coming up."

"You forgot about Christmas?"

Her utterly shocked expression was far too amusing. "This may come as a shock to you, but I haven't celebrated Christmas with anyone in about seven years or so."

"*Seven years!?* But why?"

"Life of a nomad, I suppose. Ever since Nana passed, it's been just me. She died on Christmas Day a ways back, so the day is bittersweet. A couple of times I had a dinner where I was employed, but those were usually hardly worth it."

"Oh, Mick." Cassidy's eyes misted with tears. "I'm so sorry to hear about your nana. You two had a special relationship."

"She was the best. Nothing feels like home without her."

She flushed at that. "So... would it be okay to ask you if you'll spend Christmas day with us? Even if just for part of the day. I know you are leaving soon, but I really don't want you to have to be alone."

Mick smiled shyly. "I'd like that."

31

Cassidy

*C*ass chewed on her nails, watching the sun come up and her eyes flicking to the front porch every few minutes. It was Christmas Day and she'd never been so nervous. Mick was set to celebrate with her family, starting with hot cocoa and Christmas donuts, then present opening, then the grand Christmas meal. It was a lot. It was a lot, a lot.

She was excited that Mick was coming over for Christmas, but her heart was breaking that he would be leaving the ranch soon after. Her attraction to him was real. And she had thought that he wanted to be with her, too. But apparently not. She'd overstepped and had paid the price. The ranch was losing a good worker, and she was losing a friend.

When he first started avoiding her after their date to the restaurant, Cass had been beside herself. She was mortified that he'd overheard what the restaurant workers had said. But he didn't want to talk about it. And she didn't want to embarrass him further by bringing it up.

She'd cried when nobody could hear her. And after a couple weeks, the sadness had turned into a dull ache.

But she didn't regret taking the chance and putting her feelings out there. She was done wallowing in what she *couldn't* do. From now on, she would take action on everything she *could* do.

Her family was trying new things too. This year was the first Christmas the family was sharing with not one, but three guests. Alejandro, Savannah and Mick, all at once. Cass couldn't explain why the idea of them being over shook her to her core. She *liked* all of them plenty. But something about the idea made her heart thunder in her chest.

Maybe she would skip the coffee part of their morning ritual.

It wasn't long before Charity joined her, dressed in Christmas themed joggers and a T-shirt. Normally they just wore their pajamas for donuts and present opening, but with guests being over... that seemed too informal. At least she could always count on her sister being on the same wavelength as her.

"Well," Charity asked after maybe fifteen minutes of sitting there, watching the first pastel rays of the sun unfurl into the cobalt sky of the fading night. "Should we get the coffee going?"

"It's still going to be probably two hours at least before anyone shows up."

"My question stands."

"You know what? Yeah. And while we're at it, why don't we heat up the fryer for the donuts?"

Charity grinned, and for a moment, it was easy to imagine that it was just like old times. "It's like you read my mind."

Together, they walked and rolled into the kitchen, Cass saving up her energy for what she knew was going to be a very long day. They started the first pot of coffee, slow brewing it and then setting out everything they'd need for the donuts. They also removed the dough from the fridge where it'd been rising or proofing—whatever Clara had said—for the past twelve hours and set that out to come to room temperature.

Naturally it was Clara who wandered in first, her hair up in curlers and rubbing the sleep from her eyes. The way her face lit up when she saw everything they'd set up was practically a present in and of itself.

"Did you guys do this just for me?"

Cass and Charity exchanged a look. "Yes. Absolutely. Just for you."

IT WAS ten AM when Mick rolled in with Alejandro and Savannah not far behind him. The donuts were delicious and crisp, matching perfectly with their mochas—or hot chocolate in Cici and Savannah's case—and the whole entire morning was absolutely lovely.

Of course, one could only hold off presents for so long, considering they had a preteen in the room. Savannah tried; she really did. It started with just her gaze flicking to the pile under the tree every few minutes. Then it shifted into her doing a walk around the living room before returning to their feast in the kitchen. Three times. Then it shifted to her just standing in front of the tree, looking intensely at the many wrapped packages.

It was just about noon, with their bellies full of sugar and caffeine, that they finally all moved to the living room with her. The house truly smelled heavenly with the turkey they had cooked overnight roasting on a low temp in the oven and Clara putting the potatoes on to boil. They'd done the Christmas meal together so many times since Mama had died that they had it down like clockwork.

"So, Savannah, you're our youngest. Do you want to be the Christmas elf?" Papa asked, his voice all warm and happy like it always was when he addressed the young girl. It was incredibly clear to Cass that he'd already adopted her as a granddaughter, and it was nice to see him have that.

"What's the Christmas elf?" she asked, her eyes practically as big as dinner plates.

"You're the person who picks out which gift someone will open. We usually go in order of oldest to youngest, but towards the end, it's usually not exactly even, so you pick the order at your discretion."

"Oh, that seems like a lot of power."

"It definitely is."

Savannah nodded resolutely, her mouth set in a determined jut. "I will do my absolute best."

"Hey, Christmas elf," Mick said, leaning in close and covering his mouth partially as if he was telling her a secret. "If you do me a solid and make sure Cassidy gets my present towards the end, an extra five dollars might end up in your stocking."

Savannah's eyes narrowed, her lips curling in an expression Cass definitely recognized as the one she wore when she was too smart for her own good.

"Make it ten and you'll have a deal."

"That's not very Christmas spirity of you."

"You're the one trying to bribe the Christmas elf."

"*Savannah*," Alejandro warned.

But Mick just held up his hand and pulled out his wallet, handing the young girl a twenty.

"I have truly learned my lesson about trying to bribe an elected official. Wink, wink."

That last part seemed to especially amuse Savannah and she let out a long laugh. "Alright, I got you, Mr. Cowboy man, wink, wink."

And just like that, it was present time.

Cass always loved watching her family open their presents. It was a pretty lengthy process considering there were six of them and they all tended to get multiple things for each other. With three new people it just made it that much more of an affair. There were socks and makeup and bolts of fabric, special hair products, the latest and greatest tools, new shoes, a plethora of little blessings all emerging from their shiny wrapping paper.

Savannah was practically beside herself, her eyes nearly bulging out of her head with every gift she received. Which definitely was more than a few, considering that everyone had gotten her about three gifts each.

And she kept to her word, leaving Mick's three presents stacked behind her. Cass tried not to eye them too much, but she couldn't help but wonder what they were. Their shape didn't really give them away and it wasn't like she'd told him what to buy. In fact, she'd never given him a wish list because she didn't really have to worry about money, while he did.

So that would make his presents all the more meaningful.

But at least she was able to forget those three boxes for a few minutes while he opened the first of her gifts.

"You didn't have to get me anything," he said with a

sheepish sort of smile over his broad features. It never failed to make her heart speed up how the intense, stern cowboy never had a problem being vulnerable around her. He'd spent a lifetime building up those walls, but he always lowered them for her. What better compliment could she ask for?

"You didn't have to get me anything," she countered right back.

"Touché," he said, giving her a look that made her toes curl even when her legs didn't want to listen to her.

"Go on," Cass said, cutting off her sibling's banter while she could. "Open it."

It was a truly massive box, about half of Mick's height, and Alejandro had to help Savannah push it over to him. Cass was practically vibrating where she was sitting, turned so she wouldn't miss a single expression that crossed his face.

He took his time, searching out each piece of tape and sliding a finger under it to peel it off. If Cass didn't know better, she would have thought that he was actively torturing her. But she realized—as she was holding her breath—that Mick hadn't had a family to open presents with in years and that it made perfect sense for him not to rush it. To savor every moment.

Goodness, even when he didn't mean to, he reminded her to be more grateful for every moment.

Finally, he had the top of the box exposed, and he reached for the box cutter they specifically had for present opening. It was like the climax of a movie as she watched the blade slide through the tape and then carefully pull off the packing material at the top.

And finally, the brand-new saddle was revealed.

Mick froze as if he'd been turned into a statue, the cutter in one hand and packing material in the other. There was complete silence in the room for a long, long moment, and

Cass had the horrible feeling that she'd done something wrong.

"Is... is this the Billy Royal Embossed Saddle?" Mick asked finally, his voice so low and quiet, like he was afraid it would all vanish if he spoke too loudly.

Cass nodded, her own throat feeling dry. Suddenly the emotion of the room was so incredibly heavy that even Savannah knew not to say anything.

"How did you know?"

Cass swallowed thickly, composing herself. "Do you remember when you were talking horses with Charlie? You said it was one of the most beautiful things that you've ever seen."

"Yeah, but it cost five thousand dollars."

She just shrugged. What was the point of money if she couldn't spoil someone who had missed so many years of getting Christmas presents?

"I can't believe you remembered that. It was just an offhanded comment."

"It wasn't offhanded to me. You don't talk about things you want very often."

When he raised his gaze to look at her, the sheer amount of emotion in his dark eyes made her knees shake. *Wow*, that was a lot. "Because I have everything I want when I'm with you."

Cass's mouth opened, then it closed, and it opened one more time, but no sound came out. Maybe on anyone else that line would have been painful, but Mick was so sincere that it made her heart swell inside of her chest.

They held each other's gaze, the moment stretching between them until Cici cleared her throat.

"Uh... is there anything else in that big ol' box?"

That seemed to jerk Mick back to reality and he looked

down at the other packaging materials. "Please tell me there isn't more," he said quietly.

"I... may have bought the entire matching tack set."

She had never really seen the cowboy move so fast, but suddenly she was in his arms, being given the best hug of her entire life.

"You're unbelievable, you know that?" he whispered into her hair, a secret just for her.

"Your bar is just really low," she countered, tilting her head up to gaze at his face again.

His expression was jam-packed with enough emotion to leave her utterly breathless. Goodness, she didn't know it was possible to love someone so much.

"Uh... do I do the next present or do we keep waiting?" Savannah asked after another moment.

That was enough to ebb some of the intensity between them, and Cass felt her cheeks color as she answered. "Feel free to keep going."

It took another hour, with Charity getting up to mash the potatoes and then Charlie going into the kitchen after her to put the sweet potatoes in the oven and take out the turkey to rest, then Cass herself scooping all the stuffing out and putting it in its own container. It was the perfect blend of their traditional schedule and making time for the three new additions to their family.

The dinner was basically ready and waiting for them when it was time for Cass to open her presents. Sitting in a wasteland of empty boxes and torn wrapping paper, her nerves started to kick up as everyone's eyes were on her.

"Here's the first box!" Savannah said, depositing it in front of her. It was surprisingly lightweight for its size, but she didn't dare to shake it to figure it out.

No, definitely no shaking. Instead, she opened it carefully, revealing an even smaller box.

"Oh, you're one of *those*, aren't you?"

Mick just shrugged, staring at her with that intense look of his. Goodness, was that how she'd felt when he'd been opening her gift? Nerve-wracking.

But she kept going, and then she was pulling out what could only be some sort of picture frame, but a large one, bigger than poster size. It was carefully covered in tissue paper and she spent another minute or so carefully unwrapping that.

"*Oh.*"

It was a painting of her, an *incredible* painting of her atop her old horse, riding across a field with her old, long hair caught in the wind. It was beautiful and full of movement, reminding her of times that had been long gone.

Her voice was thick in her throat when she spoke again. "Did you paint this?"

He nodded. "I did."

Seemingly having learned from the last time, Savannah hurried to hand her another present. This one was longer and thinner, and Cass quickly opened it as a distraction from the emotions swirling through her.

She loved the painting, she did. But it also reminded her of how much she'd lost. It'd been ages since she'd been on a horse, and that made her heart ache in direct contrast with all the good feelings from earlier.

"I didn't know you were an artist."

"I dabble from time to time."

"Right."

She finished opening the second present and it revealed a cane. But not any cane, rather a beautiful one carved out of some sort of reddish wood and polished to a glistening shine.

The handle was exceptional too, with a padding that felt like memory foam. It really was exceptional.

...but it was another reminder of her accident.

Mick must have seen the reaction on her face. "I know that you tend to look on most of your mobility aids with disdain, but I wanted you to have something you could be proud of. Something gorgeous and stylish, rather than something you tolerate."

Oh.

That was nice. And it *was* truly a magnificent thing. It looked like some sort of valuable relic that would have been passed down through generations instead of the black and gray practical one she had.

"Are you ready for the last one?"

Cass nodded, not trusting her voice, and Savannah passed her a box that was almost identical to the first. She took her time on this one, trying to gather herself and also fight the conflicting emotions in her chest. His presents were just so *good*, why did she have to react so viscerally to them? She had thought she'd come to terms with her accident, but clearly not as much as she'd imagined. And why did he put so much effort into these presents when he was leaving?

With shaking hands, she removed the last of the tissue paper to reveal... another painting of her on her horse?

She opened her mouth, about to spout off her confusion, but then she realized exactly what was happening. The painting was similar to the first, but not the same. Her hair was shorter, her frame was thinner and softer, and she could ever so faintly see some scarring on her exposed arms. It was her, after her accident, but riding a horse just like she had before.

"I believe in you, Cass," Mick said, voice low and rumbling. "I know you've lost so much, but I know that won't defeat you."

Cass's heart thundered in her chest and she looked at the three gifts again, all of it clicking in her head.

Her past.

Her present.

Her future.

All of them beautiful, all of them one of a kind. Mick didn't have a lot of money, sure, but that clearly didn't matter. Somehow, he'd given her everything that she didn't even know to ask for.

She didn't know what luck she had for him to have stumbled into their lives, but she would be forever grateful. She had been surviving before, sure, trudging towards her recovery out of sheer spite. But Mick? Mick made her want to live just to *live*. To have joys and hopes and things to look forward to.

He'd saved her, and he didn't even know it.

"Thank you," she said, throwing her arms around his neck.

"Well," Clara said, her tone warm and full of understanding, and clearly trying to give them some alone time. "I don't know about the rest of you, but I am *starving*. Let's all head into the dining room, shall we? Oh, and Charity, help me in the kitchen, would you?"

Classic Clara, always looking out for everyone else. The family all exited, leaving Cass and Mick alone as they stared into each other's eyes.

"Did I do right by you, Cassidy?" Mick asked, the smallest of smiles around those full lips of his.

"You did perfectly," she whispered.

"Cassidy..." Mick said, looking into her eyes. "Why did you buy me that expensive saddle when you know I'm leaving? When people think less of your family for having me here?"

"Don't you know?" Cassidy said, looking at him from under her lashes.

"Know what?"

"Mick, it doesn't matter what other people think," Cassidy said, laughing and shaking her head. "My goodness, in case you haven't noticed, we kind of do our own thing here on the Miller Ranch. It is much more important to be yourself than to be what someone else expects of you."

"Huh," Mick said, then hesitated. "I never thought of it that way."

Cassidy saw the confusion on his handsome face. Had that been why he wanted to leave? Not because he wasn't attracted to her but because he didn't want to be a burden to her family. Huh. A rush of heat ran through Cassidy's body. She had to tell him.

"And besides," she said, looking directly at him and sitting tall. "I love you."

The words hit him with all the weight that one would expect, and for a moment he couldn't breathe. But not for a bad reason, but because his heart was so full, his happiness so intense, that there just wasn't room for anything as pesky as oxygen.

"I love you too, Cassidy."

At that she tilted her head for a kiss.

She kissed him once, twice, three times before pulling away to look over his beautiful face again. "Who would have guessed you'd turn into my Christmas cowboy?"

He chuckled at that. "Is that what I am now?"

"Well, you certainly are a gift."

"Pfft, alright now, I'm cutting this off before we get any cheesier. Let's join the rest of your family."

And together they joined the others in the living room for their first Christmas meal together.

The first of many, she hoped.

EPILOGUE: MICK

Two Months Later

"Alright, are you ready?"

Cassidy swallowed thickly, looking up at Othello's tall side. "I..." Her intense eyes flicked to him, but they were filled with a trepidation that he wasn't used to seeing.

Mick's eyes softened as he caught her gaze. "You know, you don't have to do this if you don't want to."

"No, no, I want to. Alejandro said I could ride a horse as long as they went as slow as possible, and you said Othello loves nothing more than going as slow as possible."

"He wants people to look at him being majestic."

"I mean, wouldn't you if you looked like that?"

Mick gave her a look of faux shock. "Are you telling me I don't look like that?" Cassidy gave him one of her looks and he was chuckling again. "You're right. I don't." Another long pause. "But really, Cassidy. We can try another day. My best friend isn't going anywhere."

"...no. I want to do it. I do. I just, uh, need a couple minutes to psyche myself up."

"You can take however long you need."

She nodded, sitting there and looking up at Othello. The horse, character that he was, just waited patiently. Mick was fully aware that his mount had infinite patience as long as he felt he was being paid proper attention to, and if he started to get restless, well, Mick had a small bag of apples for a reason.

"Alright. I'm ready."

"Are you sure?"

"Yeah. Now help me get up before I lose my nerve, please."

"You've got it."

His hands went to her waist, providing lift as she walked up the mini steps then swung her leg over Othello's wide back. It took her considerable effort and Mick didn't miss her grunt, but she made it with only a tiny shove from him.

"I can't believe I'm up here," Cassidy said, her eyes going wide as she looked around. "I haven't ridden a horse in over a year. I..." Her voice cracked, and that sound went straight through to his heart. The things Cassidy had lived through... had fought through. She was a warrior in every sense of the word.

When she spoke again, her voice was barely a whisper. "I thought I'd never be able to ride again."

Mick didn't say anything, because although he wanted to comfort her, he also knew that it wasn't his place. She was processing something, and she only needed him to stand still and be there for her.

And if that was what she needed, then Mick was fine with standing there for just about forever. He may not have been much of a planner, but he sure was patient.

"Alright," she said, straightening up and looking forward.

Mick waited for the command to go, but Cassidy seemed lost in thought again, her intense stare on the stable doors.

"Are you ready to start?"

No answer for a long moment, then another one, but then she finally nodded. "Let's try a slow walk around the building."

"Sounds perfect." He gave Othello a loving pat on his side. "You treat my lady right, you hear?"

The horse gave him a look as if to question if there was any other option, then slowly plodded forward.

Most people didn't realize it actually took quite a lot of discipline for a horse to go slowly. Even a lazy horse wanted to go at the pace of their natural gate. But Othello was a champion and, despite his rough start, he had a knack for reading his rider unlike any mount that Mick had ever met.

Cassidy rocked for a minute, like her hips got caught on the natural sway of riding in the saddle, and for a moment she slipped to the side. But she managed to right herself without Mick's help and then they were out the door.

"I'd forgotten what this felt like," she said, a strange expression on her face.

Mick could pick out happiness, sadness, joy, and so much pain written across her features. What all was she thinking of? What memories were going through that mind of hers? He wished he could wipe them all away, but that wasn't how life worked. Just like he had a scar at the center of his chest, she would bear her scars for the rest of her life, both physically and mentally.

"I'm glad that you could remember again."

Her head turned to him and *oh*, if there wasn't just so *much* in the depth of her eyes. Once more, he was overwhelmed and caught up with everything that she was. Cassidy was a force of nature, a testament to perseverance, and he couldn't believe he was lucky enough to be a part of her journey.

"You know," she murmured softly as Othello kept carefully, ever so carefully, plodding along. "I've been thinking..."

Mick normally might have teased her, made a reference or joked, but he could feel that it wasn't the time. "About?"

"Well, everything, but specifically about making a difference." Mick nodded, showing that he was listening but knew that she didn't need his input quite yet. "I realize that I have so *much*. I mean, sure, my life hit a hitch and things haven't been *easy*, but I can't imagine how much worse it would be if we weren't wealthy. My lift, the wheelchair ramp, my collapsible walker, all of that were bought or made for me before I even got home because my family could.

"And if I'd needed anything else, well they would have gotten me that too. How much harder would everything had been if I was stuck in just my bedroom? Or if I was trapped on a single floor? Would I have fallen down the stairs even more often or just been sequestered in my own misery?"

"I suppose that's all possible," Mick said when he realized she was looking for a response.

"Exactly. And that's not right. It's hard enough going through a traumatic event without having to worry about the financial aspect of it. So, I was thinking, I want to do something about it."

"Something like what?"

"Well, I'm talking to our lawyers, but I'm thinking of starting a foundation to provide mobility aids and accessibility measures to people in need. Old, young, you name it. We'd start in this county, then go from there.

"We'll start small, of course, walkways and ramps up into homes and accessible bathtubs, but I want to expand into wheelchair-friendly transports for schools, maybe a ride service for doctor appointments, and chair lifts or wheelchair elevators like I have.

"There will be bumps, and I realize a lot of the people we'll be helping will have apartments, not their own homes, and that will present its own set of problems, but I want to—no, I *need* to do something. I can't help but feel like I should make something good out of all that has happened. My eyes have been opened to a whole world I'd otherwise know nothing about."

Her gaze flicked back to him and once more, her expression was open and vulnerable. Mick had been around Cassidy long enough to know that was quite the special expression, one usually only her family members got to see when she was at her weakest. He cherished deeply that she trusted him with that, and he was working on his own walls too. They were mostly down with her, of course, but occasionally a weird barrier would pop up and he'd have to examine why he felt that way and how the block had gotten into place.

"I think that's brilliant," he said, offering his hand up to her. She took it, slightly releasing her death-grip on the reins, and he kissed the top of it. "If anyone could do it, it's you."

"That means the world to me, you know. I really value your opinion, Mick."

"I don't understand why, but I'm not going to question you."

"Good, you've learned."

"I've been told I'm capable of that once in a very great while."

She laughed, and it was such a sweet sound that Mick joined in with a small chuckle of his own. Sometimes, if he hung around Cassidy for too many hours in a row, his cheeks would cramp from all the smiling and his abs would be lightly sore. It was the best workout he'd ever had, if he was honest.

"So you don't think it's crazy?"

"No. I think it's entirely practical, and the right thing to do. You're right. You do have resources that a lot of people don't, resources that could really change someone's life."

"Do you wish you would have had more resources with your nana? That you'd grown up differently?"

"I suppose it would have been nice for that to have been a realistic opportunity. To be like a regular kid, but I can't say things would have turned out any differently." He looked to Othello, his right-hand man and loyal companion. His rock that had gotten him through some rough times. The only family he'd had for years. "The moment I met this guy, my fate was kind of sealed to become a cowboy. I think I've always been meant for the land, fixing things and..." He glanced back to the love of his life, sitting proud and noble on top of Othello's back. "Taking care of people."

Cassidy smiled that special smile at him, the one that made his toes curl within his boots. "As long as you let me take care of you, too."

Mick helped her down from his horse.

His heart was just so overwhelmed with all of the good from the moment. He was at peace but also excited for their future. He was full of desire, but also just wanted to be still and enjoy their moment for what it was. He wanted to spend the rest of his life with the woman in his arms, but he also wanted time to never pass, so they could stay this happy forever, nothing changing.

But most of all, he had a goal. He had a *purpose*. That empty spot that had been inside him since Nana had passed was filled with something perfect and comforting.

"I will never stop thanking God for the day he made me run into your sister," he murmured before kissing her silly. Her head, her forehead, her cheeks, the tip of her nose and finally her lips were all his target, being lavished with little pecks that never failed to make her giggle and blush. She let him though, and when he did reach her mouth, she kissed him right back.

"Are you sure you don't mind giving up your plans to move west?"

Oh Cassidy. His beautiful, wonderful, loyal Cassidy. What had happened to make her so sure that people would eventually leave or turn on her?

"There were never any plans." He saw the sharp look she gave him, as if she didn't believe him. "There weren't, really. That was one of the things I was struggling with. The only reason I kept going further and further west was so I could find a home that finally felt right."

"Oh!" She breathed heavier, her eyes growing wider. "And... and you've found that?"

Mick nodded, leaning over one more time to kiss her cheek. "I have. Right here on the Miller Ranch."

"Amen," she said and chuckled with joy, just like he'd hoped. "Only moving forward from now on for the two of us."

"Together?" Mick asked, trying to keep his voice level.

Cassidy squeezed his hand, understanding everything that he wasn't saying. "Together. Always."

Well. Mick could certainly work with that.

EPILOGUE: CASSIDY

The Week before Christmas, Ten Months Later

"You'll tell me if you're gonna start a food fight, right? You *have* to tell me if you're about to start a food fight!"

Cass gave her youngest sister, Cici, a real big-sister glare. "Don't you get enough drama off at college?"

"Please, the only drama we get is two girls liking the same guy. That's *nothing* compared to family drama. I can't believe you guys had a whole throw down at Simon's party and I was home sick with the flu."

"Cici, that was literally almost three years ago, and they've really turned it around." That was absolutely true. Ever since Cass's accident, the McLintoc Millers that they'd been estranged from had reached out. Not all at once, but it had been the sons first and, after nearly six months, their father. In fact, he was the one who shelled out for the moped as a gift. It wasn't necessary, of course, they all had plenty of money, but it had been an obvious olive branch that Cass didn't have trouble accepting.

Cici rolled her eyes, ever the twenty-three-year-old she was. "You know, things are much less exciting when you're all mature about stuff."

"Oh no. What a shame," Cass said with the utterly flattest tone she could manage.

"Keep going like that and I'll steal your cane."

"You're more than welcome to try it."

Cici narrowed her eyes, getting that look on her face that only a littlest sibling could have. What was it about being the youngest that filled a human with mischief incarnate?

"You know it's in very bad form to bully a disabled person. Don't they teach that at college?"

"Fine, *fine*. But you—"

She was interrupted by two blonds that looked like Marilyn Monroe. Huh, Clara would fit right in with them.

"Hello there!" the one with her hair in a bun said, smiling effortlessly. Oh. Wow. She was friendly and had killer biceps. "You're Cassidy, right? I heard about the charity you're running, and I've got a proposal for you I think you might like!"

"Hey," the other blond said, her curls a wild mane around her head. "You want to introduce us before you start saving the world?" She had a deeply southern drawl that sounded like a more intense version of Mick's accent. Granted, his was pretty mild considering he only had it from traveling around the lower half for ten years, give or take.

"Oh, right. Sorry. I'm Missy and this is Virginia. I'm married to Bart."

"And I'm engaged to Samuel. If I recall right, you lot had a bit of a row at the last shindig."

Cass flushed lightly at that.

"That was mostly Charity, but yeah, it was certainly an event."

"And I missed it!" Cici piped up from beside her, hand already thrust out. "I'm Cecilia, but you can call us Cass and Cici, respectively. I'm the youngest of the whole family, so feel free to spoil me."

Cici could be a lot for some people. She was bright and enthusiastic about everything she did, easily slipping into long monologues about one special interest or another. Not too unlike Savannah, actually, so maybe that was why the young preteen fit so well into their natural family dynamic.

"Spoil you?" Missy said with a crinkle to her grin. "Please don't talk to my daughter. I don't want her picking up that tactic."

"Like she needs to," Virginia joked. "Her daddy gives that child everything she could ever want. She barely knows who anyone else is, those two are so glued together."

Missy laughed and it was a pleasant, boisterous sound. Cass had seen her around once or twice, but she'd never really talked to the tall woman. She'd always wanted to, considering that Missy had also stood up against McLintoc Miller during that fateful graduation dinner, but...well, just another thing that the accident had thrown off.

"That's alright. At least little Ricky is a mama's boy. But anyway, now that we're introduced, I heard that you run a foundation to help lower-income people get mobility aides, and I run an animal shelter and rescue program that covers three states. However, I've been wanting to expand and get into both emotional support animals and service animals for the underprivileged. Considering that most people who need your services also might need mine, I was really interested in talking about whether a partnership might work out for us."

Oh *wow*. That was certainly just about the last thing that Cass had expected. "Yeah, there's a huge crossover there. I'd *love* to talk about that."

"Yes! That's awesome. Let me give you my number and we'll chat later. It's Christmastime after all, but I wanted to at least float the idea to you while I had you. Maybe, if you stay long enough, I can show you one of my shelters!"

"That sounds great."

There was more chatting as they exchanged conversation, but then children were running up and demanding the attention of both the women. The duo was dragged away, with Charity walking up as they exited.

"Goodness, those little ones are precious," she murmured, hand on her stomach. Cass didn't miss the bit of melancholy to her tone. She was well aware of her sister's fertility issues and the unanswered longing she had for a little one. "I just wanna gobble them all up."

"I do not recommend eating our cousins' children," Cici said, excusing herself with a bow. "Especially since we all just started talking again."

"You know, that's some solid advice," Mick said, coming up from behind Cass and gently putting his arm over her shoulder. "How are you holding up, by the way?"

Cass sent him the warm grin that she always seemed to wear around him. It'd been a year and a half since they'd started dating and he still was just as gentlemanly as when they'd started. He'd also been with her through every milestone and set back of her recovery, so he knew better than anyone when she was reaching her limit.

Thankfully, she was nowhere near it, even though she was surrounded by almost a hundred people of various relations. It helped that she was having the time of her life. She'd forgotten how much she loved hanging out with her extended family.

It also helped that the Millers had really gone all out setting up the Christmas dinner. The family had gotten just *too* big to fit into their sizable home, so they'd set up a heated sort of enclosed pavilion outside for the big dinner and present exchange. As for sleeping arrangements, well, all their sons' abandoned rooms were chock full of guests, along with their sons' current houses. For everyone else not willing to stay in either of those, well the one inn in town was certainly experiencing a mighty uptick in business.

"I'm perfectly fine, but I wouldn't mind finding a seat and helping myself to some of their appetizers."

"I did notice they had a real spread. You said your Aunt Annie made all of this?"

"I mean, she probably had help from others, but she's the mastermind. If there ever was a hostess, it was her."

"Actually," Charity added. "Aunt Liz made a lot of the baked goods with that Nova woman. Heard they came up two days early."

"Nova?" Cass asked, racking her brain. "Which one is that again?"

"The leggy British woman."

"Right, right! I thought she was the tiny, pregnant one with the big grin."

"No, that's uh... Frenchie, I think?"

Mick huffed from beside her as they walked. "I don't know how any of you keep all these names straight. You practically have a whole city here."

Cass looked around at the crowd spread out in the massive pavilion plunked right in front of Aunt and Uncle Miller's house, snow swirling outside of the acrylic windows in some of the panels. It was a stark contrast, the comfort and welcoming nature of the inside compared to the frigid Christmas weather outside. "We really did have a boom. Would you believe that just seven years ago, every single one of us was single? The Miller families were a real broken-hearts club."

As she said that, three different children ran in front of them, all with different colored heads of hair and features. Life sometimes had a real sense of humor.

"That, uh, that is real hard to believe."

"We Millers move fast, I guess."

They continued to chat as she moved to one of the tables they'd set up, and then Mick was walking off to get her a plate and drink. Of course, Cass wasn't alone for even a minute, with plenty of family members swinging by.

It seemed that their family really was doing better than ever. Not everyone was there, of course. Charlie was off with a traveling rodeo while Alejandro and Savannah had stayed behind because of the flu season and his work was extra demanding. Clara had also stayed behind, volunteering herself to tend to the animals.

Some of Cass's other cousins were missing as well, like one of the twins whose wife was far too pregnant to travel, and the youngest of Aunt and Uncle Miller who was in another country on business and his wife was with her family in Hawaii, where he would be expected to join them for the holidays.

But even with a handful or two of people missing, the entire tent was filled with laughing, eating and plenty of merriment. There were no grudges, no unspoken resentment. Even McLintoc Miller himself wasn't grumbling about bleeding hearts or how much Aunt and Uncle Miller wasted on spoiling their animals.

A few years ago, she would have assumed such a thing would have been impossible, but there they all were, gathered together under love and support and a really impressive industrial heater. Cass didn't even want to think about how much power that thing was sucking up.

Yikes.

Not that they had to worry about bills, as it were. But ever since dating Mick, Cass had become more aware of what it was like for the layperson and being cognizant of bills. She liked to think it was another way he made her a more well-rounded person.

Eventually, more and more people began to sit, ready to fill their bellies with warm, delicious food. Cass had already been grazing for a while, so she was free to watch, and she didn't miss how Mick suddenly stood up and walked over to the main banquet table. His plate was still half full, so he couldn't be getting more food. What was he—

"Hello, friends, family and everything in between," he said, raising his hands.

"What is he doing?" Cass hissed, feeling her stomach drop out from under her.

"Well, why don't you listen?" Papa said with a chuckle, a knowing sort of sparkle to his eyes. Cass looked to Charity, who was smiling so brightly she practically glowed and there were tears beginning to fill her eyes.

Wait...

What?

"Some of you know me, but most of you don't. My name is Michael Jones, but people know me as Mick, and I'm one of the lucky ones who has been welcomed into your wild, very big family with open arms." There was a cheer from the wives, fiancées and girlfriends, which had Cass looking around. Huh, there really was an awful lot of them. "And I'm aware this is Christmas and not Thanksgiving, but I just wanted to take a moment and tell you how truly grateful I am for Cassidy Miller."

Oh no, why would he do that? Sure, Cass liked compliments as much as the next person, but that was very different from having someone announce praises about her in front of all of her relatives during their Christmas get-together. Yikes.

"I have never seen anyone as strong, or as persistent, as one Cassidy Miller," Mick said, those dark eyes of his landing right on her. "She had persevered against what would have stopped other people in their tracks, and I've been lucky enough to be with her on part of her journey.

"I know that she tends to downplay her accomplishments, but I won't. I've watched my love going from barely being able to get around to being able to walk with only a cane to support her. And, despite having so much of her schedule taken up by everything she needed to do to keep up her health, she's also been helping others and changing their lives."

He was really overselling it. Cass felt her cheeks coloring. What *was* he doing?

"I will be the first to say that I am always in awe of Cassidy, and I am entirely aware that I do not deserve her. But even though she is infinitely out of my league, I know without a doubt that I want to spend the rest of my life by her side if she'll let me."

He was kneeling, oh gosh! He was *kneeling*! And then his hand went behind him, and he pulled a small blue box from his pocket.

He was... he was...

"Cassidy Miller, I know that I'm still learning and growing

to be someone deserving of you, but would you give me the perfect Christmas present by marrying me anyway?"

She couldn't breathe. She couldn't even *speak*. Joy overflowed through her, lifting her to her feet and sending her over to him before she'd even known she moved. "Yes! Absolutely, *yes!*" she cried, letting her cane drop and flinging her arms around his shoulders.

He caught her, pulling her against his strong front and nearly crushing her to him. But she loved it and didn't want him to stop. If she had her way, he'd just hold her forever and ever.

"I love you," she whispered before kissing him with all she had, the cheers and whoops from her family taking a backseat to everything that was Mick. He kissed her back, and it was like her soul straight left her body and propelled into the stratosphere.

When they parted, he slid the ring onto her finger, not an easy feat considering that her hands were shaking so hard. But instead of being from muscle cramps or pain, it was because she was so happy. No, happy didn't even cut it. She was overjoyed, ecstatic, and so utterly in love that she couldn't imagine ever going back to how she'd been before.

And she wasn't going to. Like she'd promised Mick all those months ago, there was only going forward for the two of them.

Forever.

But for the moment, she was going to enjoy her cowboy and the best Christmas she'd ever had.

∾

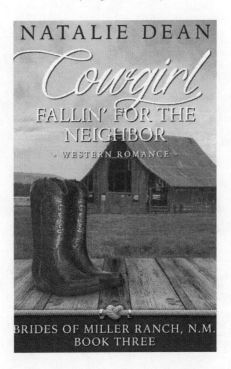

Hello readers! I hope you enjoyed Cassidy and Mick's love story. Next in the line-up is another one of my favorites. This one is a beauty and the beast type romance. Although Clara is a bit heavy-set, she's a beautiful woman and has a heart of gold. Nathan, on the other hand, is handicapped and as bitter as they come. Clara doesn't let that stop her from helping him out though, it wouldn't be the right thing to do to just let him be.

You can find Clara and Nathan's journey to love on all major retailers. But of course, as previously mentioned, it sure would be great if you could support my small bookstore. Scan the QR code below (might be on the next page, depending on the book format) to be taken to Cowgirl Fallin' for the Neighbor at Natalie Dean Books. If scanning QR codes isn't your thing, you can find my store here: nataliedeanbooks.com Just look under the Miller stories tab for Brides of Miller Ranch, N.M., and you should be able to find this book.

ABOUT THE AUTHOR

Born and raised in a small coastal town in the south, I was raised to treasure family and love the Lord. I'm a dedicated homeschooling mom who loves to travel and spend time with my growing-up-too-fast son.

When I'm not busy writing or running my business, you can find me cleaning house, cooking dinner, feeding our three rescue cats, trying to make learning fun and coaxing my son to pick up his toys. On less busy days, you may also find me paddling down a spring run in Florida, hiking a mountain trail in Georgia (on the rare vacation to the mountains), or enjoying a book.

If you love Natalie Dean books, you can be notified of new releases by signing up to my newsletter at nataliedeanau thor.com, where you will also receive two free short stories for signing up. Just click on the "Free Books" tab at the top and you'll be on your way!

Also, as previously mentioned, I've opened my own online bookstore and I'd love your support! As of June 2024, I'm selling my ebooks at Natalie Dean Books. By late summer or fall 2024, I should have audiobooks, regular paperbacks, large print paperbacks, dyslexic print paperbacks and signed paperbacks all available. At the request of my loyal readers, I'll also be adding merchandise, such as glasses, cups, magnets and more. So come check out my small mom-owned author business at nataliedeanbooks.com.

You can also scan the QR code below to be taken to the home page of Natalie Dean Books.

f facebook.com/nataliedeanromance

Made in the USA
Columbia, SC
26 October 2024

44756409R00155